Changed Fate

35+   40-↙

40↙

Asfaw Legesse

አሳታሚ እና ማከፋፈያ ኃላ/የተ/የግ/ማ
PUBLISHING AND DISTRIBUTION PLC

Mega Publishing and Distribution PLC 2019

Mega Publishing and Distribution PLC 2019

☎ 011-1-23 29 09
011-1-23 29 05
011-1- 23 29 06
011-1-232912-16

✉ 9144
Addis Ababa
Ethiopia

Website: www.megabooksplc.com
Email: publishing@megabooksplc.com

Chapter 1

It was dark as usual when I arrived home. I had gone first, as always, to the nearby Saint Gabriel Church, which was about a kilometer away from my home. The church was a circular building made of red bricks. Hollow round tin rods the size of a finger and small tin crosses hanging around surrounded the circular corrugated tin roof and clicked when blown by the wind. The church had a porch, the ceiling of which was decorated with traditional church paintings; paintings of saints with wide open eyes and Afro hair. The inside ceiling of the church was also decorated with similar spiritual paintings. The church compound was spotted with old indigenous trees that were rarely seen out of the compound. It was usually quiet around the church, except the occasional sounds of monkeys and baboons playing or fighting around. The silence made the church and its surrounding area majestic, a perfect place to worship God. I often sat under a tree. I prayed, sang and praised the Lord sitting there alone. I felt the presence of God and my heart was filled with joy.

The church was surrounded by a natural forest that is dense in the immediate vicinity, but becomes less and less dense as one goes down to the Gumri River. And on the other side of the river is our village, set in an open field. I live with my family in a camp of Ayehu Agricultural Development, a private commercial farm in Ankasha Guagussa Wereda, Awi Zone, Amhara Region. The atmosphere is often loud at the camp, and the quiet of the church was a refuge for me.

I attended Yessenbet Timhirt Bet, the Sunday school as we call it, even though it was held every day of the week. Young girls and boys who were about my age and a few adults and young men who were leaders of the Sunday School including Kassa, Gizaw and Yared met daily around five in the evening and usually stayed there singing songs, rehearsing plays, or listening to someone among us preaching until six-thirty or seven pm. Those who hadn't known how to beat drum learnt how to play the big church drum.

Near the church there was a spiritual school called Ye'Zema Timhirt Bet, where boys who were destined to become deacons and priests studied melodies composed by Saint Yared around 519 AD.

At our school we studied half of the day. There was morning and afternoon shift, so some students attended school in the morning and others attended in the afternoon. The shift changed weekly. If I were on the morning shift this week, I would be on the afternoon shift next week. When I was on the morning shift, I would have a chance to go to church earlier. I would enjoy listening to them singing for several hours. When I was in the afternoon shift, class would end at five o'clock and I would not waste any minute waiting for my friends. I would be in very much hurry to go to church. I did not even worry to have snack. I would rather starve than miss the few minutes of pleasure I get listening to the students' songs. I hastily changed my school uniform; wore a longer skirt; draped myself in netela and dashed out of our house to the church.

Sitting under the shade of a tree in the church compound, I listened to the boys singing until our program began. The melody filled my heart with indescribable joy. I felt as if I were in a heavenly place. The students worshiped, adored, and praised God for His mercy and generosity, for His might and sovereignty. I felt that the birds sang and the trees danced together with the students. I believed the colobus monkey jumped from one tree to another in the forest because it was overjoyed by the heavenly melody. And the monkey, with its beautiful black and white hair, looked like a monk that put on a black cloak, a monk's white shemma and a black hat. When I listened to those sweet spiritual melodies, I felt sad that I was a girl. I envied boys. The melody school was open only for boys who were expected to serve the Ethiopian Orthodox Church as deacons, priests, or other higher spiritual leaders.

When I arrived at our house, it was a few minutes past seven. I saw my father at the door of our hut holding a thin stick in his hand. I did not like the way he looked at me. I could see that he was angry and I thought that my sisters must have made some mistake to annoy him. I did not panic or worry about his anger as I had not done anything wrong.

"Emebet, where are you coming from?" he asked me angrily as I approached him.

"From the church," I replied gently.

I was still wearing my headscarf, my netalla was draped over my back, and the hems crossing at my shoulders. It was obvious that I had been at church.

'What were you doing at the church until this time?" he fumed.

"I was rehearsing the songs and a drama that the Sunday school is going to present for the upcoming festival," I answered confidently for I knew my father did not have any reason to be upset about my going to the church.

"Why don't you spend the whole night there?"

My father had never scolded me even if I stayed late at the church. What happened to him this evening? I wondered.

"If you ever go to church except on Sundays, I will do what I have to do," my father continued wagging a finger at me.

I gazed at him quietly, unable to believe that my father threatened me for going to church. Someone must have upset him today, I thought. Otherwise, he would not be angry with me just for staying at the church until dusk. Or had someone misinformed him, told him they saw me somewhere else?

"I didn't go anywhere else. I was at the church." I said.

"I know that you did not go anywhere else. Have you heard what I said Emebet?" he shouted.

Then, he paused for a moment. "You can't raise a foot to go to church except on Sundays! Is that clear?"

He liked my being a religious person. What made him change his mind now? I thought, but did not say a word.

A few minutes later, when I thought his anger subsided, I approached him once more.

"Father, what is wrong if I go to church?"

My father jumped to his feet and picked up a stick. He beat me on my back and butts. I folded my legs a bit to cover my legs with my dress lest he hit me on my unprotected legs. "Daddy why do you beat me? I have just asked to know why you do not want me to go. What else did I say? Please, Father. Don't beat me!" I begged him trying to protect myself with my hand in vain. My father rarely punished me this way.

"You don't listen to me."

"I do listen to you, Father. I do."

"You do not listen. You will not listen to me." He tried to avoid my hands and beat me on my shoulders and back. It was painful.

I kneeled in front of him and held the stick firmly. "I do listen to you, Father. Please don't beat me." I looked up to him and beseeched him.

He yanked the stick out of my hand and beat me twice. "Do you mean that I should not go to church?"

"Yes."

He stopped beating me and said, "Yes, I don't want you to go to what you call the Sunday School."

In the evening, the mood in our house was not good. My father sat on our only chair, a stern look on his face. My mother also sat on a stool near the kitchen door. Her face was gloomy. She looked as if she was rewinding our today's confrontation in her mind. My younger brother and two sisters had also overheard the argument between my father and I, and they still looked shocked. Silence prevailed in the house as all of us were thinking on our own. I pulled out an exercise book from my school bag and began reading, but I could not concentrate. I could not understand a single sentence I read. I was totally distracted by the difficult situation I was in. My father turned on the radio but I could tell that he was not listening. Every now and then, he rubbed his forehead with his palm as he usually did when he was very upset. He turned off the radio after a while.

My mother said to me, "Give him water for his hands."

I brought him a jug of water and a bowl. He snatched the bowl and the jug from my hands and put it on the floor. He was too angry to even let me pour water on his hands. I went back to my seat. He began washing his hands.

"Let me help you." My sister Sossina jumped to her feet.

"No," he growled.

As the eldest child, I always ate dinner with my parents, but today they had not let me eat with them. When I moved to the table, my father threw his hand in the air and snapped, "Go, eat with your sisters!"

I was confused. I tried to eat dinner with my brother and two sisters, but I did not have appetite. My gaze darted across the room as if to find the explanation of my parents' behavior from the walls and furniture. There were many cracks in the round wall made of wood that was plastered with mud mixed with straw, but they were not visible now as it was dark outside and the room was dimly lit by a single kerosene lamp. In one corner, I saw my parents' bed covered with an old blanket that had become as thin as bed sheet and should have been out of service long ago. In front of the bed, across the room, there was a raised floor made of stone and mud, which we call *medeb*. My siblings sat on it now. The floor was covered with two sheep skins which served as our sofa during the day and a bed for my sister Sossina and me at night. A rolled up cow skin was laid on the floor next to the *medeb*. My younger brother and sister, Workneh and Yemisrach slept on it at night.

Feeling lost and betrayed I looked at our house differently. We often cooked food with firewood and, since our living room and kitchen area were only separated by a short wall made of mud and wood, there was soot everywhere. A dirty shelf, blackened with edible oil and soot, stood next to the kitchen door. There were several cans, jars, glasses, and bottles on the shelf. Some of them contained *berberie* (powdered red pepper), *shiro* (the flour of peas and beans), salt, butter, and edible oil. The ceiling, held up by a big wooden pillar in the middle of the hut, was also covered with soot. I felt as if my whole world had been darkened by the betrayal of my parents.

My parents loved me very much. My mother called me lovingly with various nicknames. My father also openly expressed his love occasionally if not always as my mother did. I was shocked to see them treating me cold heartedly as if I was their enemy. Why were they acting this way?

Late that night, I lay on the *medeb* next to Sossina. Normally I was comforted by her soft, rhythmic breathing next to me, but tonight I couldn't sleep wondering what happened to my parents to be this much angry with me.

The next day after school I went back to church. I made sure to arrive home before dark for I did not want to have another confrontation with my father. But my father was waiting for me when I returned. He was furious that I had disobeyed him and he shouted at me for several minutes, throwing his hands in the air and bumping our table with his fists, causing it to shimmer and shake on its unstable legs.

I stood behind the table trembling with fear.

"But Father, I like going to church. What is wrong with it? It's good to go to church." I said. I couldn't understand why he suddenly became so averse to my going to church during the week.

"You are a student and you need to focus on your studies. And I heard there are some bad people around the church these days."

"Bad people?" I was surprised. "There are only people who fear God."

"Shut up!" he snapped. "I said you don't go to church except on Sundays."

It was rare that may father shouted and acted like that. I was confused but one thing was sure, he had given me a strict warning not to go to church, and I would have to try to obey him.

Chapter 2

I did not go to church for few days to show my father that I was obedient to him, but those few days were difficult ones. I desperately missed going to church. I could sing at home, but how could I survive without listening to the sweet songs of the students of the spiritual melody school? The days became long and boring.

I sat on a grass field next to the dusty volleyball field, my back to the students playing volleyball. A friend of mine, Senait, came over and sat next to me.

"You're brooding. What is wrong with you?" she asked.

"Nothing." I said without looking at her. I was not interested in talking to anyone.

"Something is wrong with you. You are not yourself. Are you unwell?" Senait asked with a look of concern over her face.

"Maybe...Maybe it was because I am not allowed to go to church," I revealed.

"I'm also sorry about that. We could not put on the play we had been rehearsing because of your absence. I was very disappointed." Senait also went to the Sunday school daily.

"What?" I was surprised. "I thought you would find someone to replace me."

"Three other girls were also absent."

"I can't believe this. Who are they?"

"Zinash, Almaz and Asnakech."

"I thought it was only me," I said covering my mouth with my hand.

"Sadly, we couldn't present the drama. I think your fathers have ganged up on us." Senait giggled.

"They must have talked to each other to make such decision at the same time."

"Do you know why they did that?" I asked.

"I think it is because of Tiringo. You know, she gave birth recently."

I nodded.

Tirngo used to go to the Sunday School regularly like Senait and me. She fell in love with Ashenafi, one of the boys at the Sunday school and everybody at the Sunday School knew that they were in love. Her parents found out and they were banned from attending the Sunday School but that did not stop them from continuing their love affair. She ended up getting pregnant.

Senait and I were silent for some time.

"Why do they think that we will end up like Tiringo?" I asked angrily.

"After all we are all girls." Senait smiled ruefully.

"How about the brothers of Zinash and Almaz? Have they not been forbidden to go to the Sunday School?"

Senait laughed. "No, they haven't. They are boys."

"I am relieved to hear this. Their absence would have created a big gap in the choir," I said.

"I wish you could come to church instead of them." Senait dropped her head.

The school bell rang letting us know the end of the recess time and we stood up and headed to class.

* * *

As soon as I got home and sat on the medeb, Sossina, who was a morning shift student, asked me to help her with washing the clothes.

"I will help you later," I said pushing her aside.

She stood in front of me and stared. "Go away!" I shouted at her. "I said I will help you later."

"You did say, 'Later' also yesterday. But I had to wash alone. Mother wants us to wash together. I have a lot of home work to do. You need to help me."

"Just go away or else I will slap you."

My mother got into the house suddenly and we kept quiet. My mother left from work early today. After half an hour, I looked for my pen to do my homework, but I couldn't find it.

"Have you seen my pen?" I asked Sossina.

"Here it is." She stretched her hand to give it to me.

"Didn't I tell you not to touch my things?" I jumped to my feet and slapped her.

My mother came running to me. She slapped me on my head. "How dare you hit my daughter?" she shouted, acting as if I were not her child. "Don't ever touch her!" she warned me.

I burst into tears. I knew I was wrong to take my anger out on my sister, but I couldn't help myself.

My mother continued to scold me. "I overheard you the other day. Why do you shout at her? It is your father who told you not to go to church, not Sossina. Leave the poor girl alone."

"I don't want her to touch my things," I said, gently sobbing.

I did not want to quarrel with my mother. I dropped my head out of remorse.

"And you didn't help her to wash the clothes, huh?"

"I was busy."

"What? What did you do to be busy? Go now and wash the clothes." My mother pushed me hard towards a bamboo basket, where we kept dirty clothes. I staggered and managed not to fall on the earthen floor.

I had frequent headaches and my heart broke. I knew I could not go on like this. I had to find some way, some innovative way, to go to church. My father was a security guard. He worked alternate days, working for twenty-four hours then resting for twenty-four hours. My mother worked in a warehouse. She did not arrive home before six in the evening. I came up with an idea. I decided to go to church when my father was on duty and return before my mother came back home.

I put my plan in motion. On most days I managed to get home before my mother came back from work. When she got home ahead of me, I hid my netela at one of my friends, carried a book, and acted as if I was returning from borrowing the book from a friend. I could go to church every other day in this way. This arrangement did not fully satisfy me, but it minimized the negative impact staying away from church had on me.

One afternoon I was about to enter our hut on my way home from church when a hand tugged at me from behind. My first thought was that my mother had arrived home ahead of me and I mentally prepared my excuse for coming home late. But I turned to see Sossina.

"What?" I asked.

"Father is asleep," she whispered quickly.

I wondered why he was at home at this time and on this day. He was supposed to return at seven the next morning.

"What happened to him?" I said lowering my voice.

"I think he is not feeling well."

"Did he ask for me?" I asked feeling guilty.

She was reluctant to answer.

"Why didn't you tell him that I went to my friend's house to study?"

"I told him so, but he ordered me to call you," she said. "Then I had to tell him that you were not at your friend's house."

"What did he say?"

"He said, 'I know what I will do when she comes.'"

I had no alternative except to confront the situation. I entered the house trembling with fear.

"Where are you coming from?" he shouted.

I was shocked and dumbfounded and in my confused state I forgot to remove my netela. Seeing the way it was draped around my shoulders, he knew at once that I had been at church.

"Emebet, I am talking to you. Why do you keep quiet?" he shouted.

"I am coming from church."

"Didn't I tell you not to go to the Sunday School?"

"Yes, you did," I said dropping my head and rubbing the hem of my netela.

"Then why did you go? Why did you not obey me?" He sat resting his back on the wall.

"I haven't done anything wrong. I just went to the church."

"You didn't do anything wrong, huh? Didn't I tell you not to go to what you call the Sunday School?"

"Father, what is wrong with going to church?" I said, looking up to him.

"You do everything on your own? You don't listen to me?"

"No, Father..."

"If you don't, why don't you obey me?" His voice softened a bit.

"I just wanted to listen to the word of God."

"You wanted to listen to the word of God?" he said sarcastically. "Is that why?"

"Yes, Father."

He stood, and unbuckling his belt he said, "But God also says that you have to respect your parents and obey them, doesn't he?"

I nodded looking at him. I was terrified when I saw him pulling his belt out and striding towards me.

He lashed me on my back with the belt. I felt my back burning.

"Please Father! Please!" I cried out.

He struck my back and thighs hard again and again.

"I am talking to you. Doesn't God say that you must obey your parents? Doesn't He?"

"Yes. ... Yes, He does. Please Father! ...I will not go there anymore," I pleaded trying to protect myself with my hands from my father's angry blows.

"Stop it! That is enough!" my mother said, standing on the doorway. Immediately as she said "Stop!" the house was flooded by a bright light. I knew it was a coincidence, my mother's entrance and the igniting of an oil lamp, yet I felt that she was an angel who came to rescue me from my father.

"Mother, please tell him to stop!" I beseeched her, feeling helpless like a small bird trampled under the heavy paws of a fierce cat.

My father was merciless. He hit me three more times before my mother came between us.

"It is enough!" my mother said.

My father did not calm down even after punishing me."Stop crying! Don't even think that this is a punishment," he shouted. "If you don't listen and obey, I'll bring out the inside of your skin to the outside. I'll break your legs and cripple you."

I dashed out of the house crying. My father followed after me and growled, "Don't cry! I will punish you more, if you don't do so. Suck it up!"

My mother rushed out and came between us again. She took me to the kitchen. My body was covered with the beating marks and bruises. Now, I did not feel guilty but rather I felt mistreated. My father was misusing his fatherhood to introduce regulations whenever he liked and to punish me severely whenever he saw minor breaches of his regulations. He had become a dictator who only wanted us to listen to his orders. I cried bitterly.

My mother tried her best to sooth me.

"Please don't cry."

"Mother, he almost killed me." I pulled the sleeves of my shirt to show her the marks left by the beating. "If you had not arrived in time, I would have been dead by now." I said sobbing.

"It is your mistake. He warned you not to go to church," my mother said gently.

"Is going to church and listening to the word of God a crime?"

"If you are not allowed to go, yes it is."

"Why? Why does this happen? This is atrocious!" I shouted.

Mother stared at me quietly and left the kitchen.

I heard her saying to my father, "Mengist, why are you so cruel to your own daughter?"

"Aster, it is you who failed to correct her in time and spoiled her so that she disobeys me."

"What did I do to spoil her?"

"When I punish her, you defend her. I don't want you to come in between us when I punish her."

"I cannot stand by while you are killing my child?" my mother said angrily.

"Just shut up!"

"Don't ever touch my child."

I heard my father shout, "Aster, how dare you speak like that to me!" and I heard some violent movements.

"Please Father, don't!" Sossina cried.

I jumped to my feet and rushed to the next room. Sossina stood between my father and mother. She was pushing our father away from our mother.

"I didn't say that you don't have to punish her. I said there should be some limit to your anger. You don't have to punish her this much," my mother said softly trying to calm him down.

"Don't tell me what I should or shouldn't do."

"Have you seen her bruises and the marks on her body?"

"Just shut up!"

"Please Father!" Sossina held his waist with her arms and tried to push him away from my mother. She was crying.

My father was very tall. In spite of his haggard face, his body was muscular and strong. He threw Sossina on to the *medeb* and strode towards my mother. She retreated quickly, but was stopped by the wall.

He held her by her neck and raised his big hand to hit her.

I darted to him and held his arm.

"You can kill me! But don't hit mother!"

He was taken aback for he thought I was still in the kitchen.

"Go away!" he said trying to free his hand. I firmly held his hand with my two hands, putting the full weight of my body into holding him back. I was stronger than both my mother and Sossina. He tried to free his arm with his other arm. I struggled with him hard. My mother jumped and held his other arm.

"I am going to scream!" mother said while holding his wrists tightly.

He hated it when mother screamed. People came from our neighborhood to see what happened. I think he came to his senses. He threw both my mother and I to different corners of the room.

"I should have killed you both," he said and left the house.

I thanked God and breathed a sigh of relief.

After that day, I stopped going to church. I missed hitting the big church drum and participating in the choir. I envied my friends who were free to attend our midweek Sunday School.

A few months passed and I heard that some of the girls who had been banned from going to the Sunday School were finally allowed to return. I was jealous when I heard two of them singing and beating the big church drum on Sunday morning at the church. I was irritated by my parents' rigidity. Senait told me that my father went to the Sunday School to check if I were going there against his will. On finding out that I was not going there, he was satisfied and stopped checking on me. The songs of the *Zema* students came across my mind and make me nostalgic. I missed beating the big church drum hanging it on my neck. After sometime, when I felt my parents no longer worried about my going to church, I started sneaking to the Sunday School sometimes.

My younger sisters informed my mother about it and my mother one day caught me. She found a whip with which to flog me.

"So you despise me? You look down at me, huh?" She was angry.

"No, I don't."

"You do. If you had not despised me, you would have obeyed me."

"Mother, I did all the work you ordered me to do."

She didn't accept this. She flogged me with the whip again.

I wept, tears ran down my cheeks.

"If you don't stop, I'll inform your father that you are beyond my control," she threatened.

I know my father is harsher and crueler than my mother. I felt that I could never go to attend the evening programs as long as I was living with my parents. *When will I be independent to do whatever I want to do?* I thought, embittered by the situation I was in. That might be realized after five or six years, too long to wait until then.

A few days later, I was sitting between my mother's legs while she was braiding my hair.

"You see the mark on my back. You hit me hard last time. How could you be so cruel?"

"You don't listen. What can I do except to punish you?" she said. I could feel that she regretted flogging me. She dropped few drops of hair oil on her hand and dabbed the mark the whip left on my back.

Encouraged by her tenderness, I said, "Mother, I do all the work you order me to do. Why don't you let me go to church? I bake injera, wash dishes and the family's clothes. I do all the work that I can."

"It is not for the household chores that we don't want to let you go to the Sunday School."

"Then, what is your reason?"

"First, you have become a poor student and your grades are slipping because you spend so much time at the church. And second, we knew there are some boys that are hovering over you. There are boys that go to the Sunday School just to prey on girls like you. Kassa is a wolf in a sheep's skin. He is going to church not because he is pious. He is after the girls there," said my mother.

"Mother, don't say that, it woud be a sin to you."

"Forget the sin." She paused and continued, "You don't know what he did?"

"What did he do?"

"Don't you know that he had affairs with Mare and Dasash?"

"I know."

"So why are you trying to protect him?" Mother stared at me suspiciously.

"That was before he started going to church. He has repented for those sins."

She chuckled and said sarcastically, "Yes, right you are. A fool raises a hyena's cub. You think he is pious? He is evil."

I did not think Kassa was a bad boy. But I did not want to argue with her, so I said, "I never trusted any of the boys."

"I heard that he is hovering over you."

I was surprised. Pointing at myself, I said, "Who? He is hovering over me? That is a big lie!"

"Don't try to deny it! I have lots of ears."

"In the name of the Father, the Son and the Holy Spirit!" I crossed my body.

"I am warning you. Just take care! I don't want anything bad to happen to you," she said wagging her finger.

"Whatever the boys say, I am not interested in them. I won't yield to them."

"Emebet, I said, you cannot go to church."

"Trust me, Mother I won't be deceived by the boys. I

can protect myself."

"No! I said no," my mother shouted, pushing me away from her.

I kept quiet now that she was annoyed.

After a while, she said, "You better not put us to shame and spoil your future."

"What do you mean?" I asked her, confused.

"Ayehu is a small village. Everything is near to everybody's eyes and ears. If people believe you are not a virgin, nobody will want to marry you."

"I don't want to get married."

"Fine. We'll see."

Chapter 3

It seemed that my parents wouldn't budge. I prayed that God would give my parents kind hearts, but God turned deaf ears to my tearful prayers.

One afternoon, I was walking from school with my friend, Matebe. We walked through the lemon and orange trees, past the side of the football pitch, and on to the road that led to our home. The dry season was about to come and the whole world around us was green and beautiful. I wished the greenery would last forever and the sun wouldn't continue to be as gentle as it was at this time; a futile wish that was aimed at stopping the cycle of nature. We walked slowly until the other students, also on their way home, were ahead of us and we could talk freely.

"What did you decide?" said Matebe.

"About what?"

"Don't you think of going again to the Sunday School?"

"I want to respect my parents' order."

"Because something bad happened to another girl, how could you stay away from the Sunday School forever? This is not fair."

"I can't do anything about it."

"No. You shouldn't give up."

"My parents do not trust me. I beseeched them. I tried to go to church hiding from them. You know the whole story. After all this effort what more can I do?"

"Maybe Satan is tempting you by using your parents to keep you away from God."

I could not believe this for two reasons. First, my parents did not want me to go to church because they hated my being pious but because they feared I would be tempted by one of the boys and end up getting pregnant. Second, they themselves were God-fearing. The church was on the way to their work place and they always devoted time to enter the church compound and pray. They attended the Holy Mass, *kidasie*, every Sunday. Satan couldn't be influencing their actions.

We walked silently for few minutes.

"I have an idea." Matebe beamed.

"What idea?"

Matebe suggested how I could cheat them and force them to let me go to church.

"Isn't lying a sin?" I asked Matebe reluctantly.

"No one would get hurt because you lied. You are not lying to cheat or hurt someone or to steal. You are lying to get closer to God and because you have a desire to serve Him."

"You think so?"

"Yes, God knows your intention and ultimate goal. He wouldn't consider this lie as a sin."

Because I was eager to go back to the Sunday School, I decided to give Matebe's idea a try.

The next day, when I returned from school I stopped twice on the way, sitting on the side of the road, acting as if I was too sick to carry my school bag and walk. I walked slowly leaning on my sister's and my friends' shoulders. When I was doing the household chores, I tightly tied my head with a headscarf and my waist with my mother's *mekenet*. When it was time for my parents to come home, I lay on the *medeb* groaning and complaining as if I was in tremendous pain and too weak to stand. I acted to convince my siblings that I was really sick.

My father brought me painkillers. I hated to take drugs so I took the tablets when they were around but I hid the tablets I should have taken in their absence.

I kept on groaning. During the day I behaved as normal, but when I met my sisters and it was time for my parents to come back home, I tightly tied my forehead with a headscarf, held my head with my two hands, and rolled in medeb moaning. Eventually, I refused to go to school. I did not attend class for a few days.

"Has the medicine not helped you?" my father asked with a look of concern on his face.

"No, it has not."

"What do you feel?"

"The pain is unbearable and it is non-stop."

My father and mother first feared that I might have malaria, then typhoid and finally typhus; the three major diseases that frequently affect the people living in Ayehu. They took me to the farm's clinic again and again. My fingers were pricked mercilessly.

I hated to give blood. When the nurse drew my blood by pricking my finger, I had to turn my head or cover my eyes with my free hand. However, I was determined to pay whatever sacrifice to make my parents believe that I was truly ill. The laboratory result revealed that I had not caught any of the most common diseases.

As Ayehu is a low land and hot area, malaria is rampant. It is common to take anti-malaria drugs even if no malaria is found in the blood and so, whenever I went to the clinic, I returned with a handful of anti-malaria tablets. Each time I was forced to take four of the ten tablets at the clinic in front of the woman who gave me the drugs. The clinics did this to discourage people from pretending to have malaria and then passing the drugs on to those who did not get free medical service at the clinics.

I detested taking the bitter malaria drugs when I really had malaria but I focused on my ultimate goal of going freely to Church. I needed my parents to believe that man-made medicine could not cure me, so I obediently took the four tablets at the clinic. I brought the remaining drugs home and I would take four of the tablets whenever they were at home, and threw the rest whenever they were away.

I kept on saying that I had a headache, and, in front of my parents, I ate very little, acting as if I had no interest in food, even though my appetite was actually very good.

One morning, I heard my parents discussing about me while lying in bed.

"What shall we do about our child? Her situation has become worse," said my father.

"Yes, it has," my mother agreed. "Her behavior is also changed."

"She does not have malaria or typhoid, yet she is getting from bad to worse. What should we do?"

"Perhaps she has been possessed by an evil spirit. Why don't we try Holy Water?"

The Holy Water my mother was speaking about was a spring, about two kilometers away from our home, that flowed by the side of a river that was found near the church. Priests prayed over the spring water and blessed it, making it holy. The water was then used to heal the sick and to force Satan and demons to leave the sick person's body.

"You better take her to the spring then," my father said.

"I can't go. I can't go near the Holy Water. I'm having my monthly period," my mother protested.

"If so, I should take my annual leave and take her," my father said.

My father and I made the long walk to the site of the Holy Water. I rested every now and then, to make father think that I was truly ill.

"Take courage. We'll be there soon," he encouraged me when I moaned and groaned. He held my waist to support me.

When we arrived at the spring, two elderly priests greeted us. They wore white turbans piled on their heads, draped their bodies with white netela and wore black rubber boots. Each of the men carried a big cross made of bronze which they used to baptize the sick with the Holy Water.

Now that we arrived, I was unexpectedly afraid to stand under the wide pipe from which the cold water flowed. I was just as reluctant to get close to the priests who stood standing and waiting. The older priest thought that I was too shy to take off my dress.

"Take it easy," the priest encouraged me.

I slipped my dress over my head and stepped under the Holy water. It was as cold as I expected. I decided to start the second part of my trick. After few seconds, I glanced around and stepped out of the flowing water. The priest shouted, "Wait! Not yet!"

I pretended I did not hear him.

"You were told to wait. Stay put," my father scolded me.

I jumped and ran away from the Holy Water wearing only my underwear.

The priest ran after me saying, "In the Name of the Father, the Son and the Holy Spirit. I command you Satan to stop! In the name of the Holy Trinity, come back! May Saint Gabriel tie you up!"

The elderly priest could not have caught up with me, but since I could not run very far wearing only my underwear, I stood still a few steps away from him. I could tell from the priest's words that he and my father thought that I was possessed by the Devil.

Another young priest came and the three of them pulled me back to the Holy Water. I struggled against them. They forced me into the Holy Water. I again tried to free my arms and ran away. They caught me and put me again under the Holy Water.

'In the name of Virgin Mary, stop what you are doing!" the priest commanded.

I twisted and twitched to pull myself away from the Holy Water. The priest tapped me on my head and on my back with the big bronze cross he was holding. He rubbed my chest around my heart and scratched my stomach with the cross.

"Who are you? I order you to speak in the name of the Holy Savior!" he ordered the Devil he thought was within me.

I kept quiet, breathing fast and deeply.

I kept this up for about three hours before I yielded and answered the priest.

"Who are you?"

"Why don't you leave me old man?" I shouted.

"Who are you?" the priest said with vigor encouraged by my answer.

"I won't tell you for you don't need to know who I am."

"I command you in the name of Saint Gabriel!"

"Wait! Why do you want to know me?"

'In the name of Saint Michael, tell me!"

I kept quiet.

"I command you in the name of Virgin Mary!" He rubbed my stomach with the cross.

"Why do you nag me Old man? Just leave me alone! Don't waste your time!" I shouted back.

"I command you in the name of the Holy Trinity!" He hit me on my head with the cross.

"Speak! Tell me!"

The blow from the cross hurt and I was now truly distressed.

"Tell me!" he continued. "Are you buda, aynetila or zar?"

"I'm buda."

"Where did you catch her?"

"At her neighborhood."

"Why did you catch her?"

"I like her face. She is beautiful. I had always wanted to catch her but she did not let me come near to her."

"How could you catch her now?"

"The fence was removed?"

"What fence?" The priest knitted his brows.

"She always went to church, sang songs and prayed there. When I finally was able to have her forbidden to go to church, she stopped singing and praying. She became vulnerable. And I caught her as there was nothing to stop me."

The priest put his cross on my forehead and pressed it hard so that I looked up. One of the other priests poured the Holy Water over my face.

"Do you hear what he said? You see what you have done to your daughter?" I couldn't see my father, but I heard the priest rebuking him.

"Now let her go! Leave her alone!" the priest commanded.

"How can I let her go after hovering around her for years? I will never let her go."

"Let her go!"

"Why hurry? I need more time."

They put me back under the pipe from which the Holy Water was pouring heavily.

"I'm burned," I screamed, although the water was still very cold. I twisted, turned, and struggled against the hands of the two priests that held me, as if I was in pain.

"Won't you leave her alone?"

"I will."

"Go ahead!"

"Okay, I will let her go, just let me out of this Holy Water."

The priests still held me under the Holy Water. The older priest's face held a serious expression as he spoke sternly to the demon he thought was inside of me. "When are you going to let her go?"

If I continued my act for longer, I would suffer more from the priest's questions and rough handling. I almost stopped but then I realized that if I yielded so soon, my father might think the whole incident was not such a big deal. I kept quiet thinking about what to say next.

"Come on! Tell me!"

Silence.

"In the name of the Holy Trinity!"

"Please don't nag me! I will leave her alone one day."

"When?"

I struggled to escape but my father and two young men held me tightly. The Holy Water was poured on me. The priest hit and rubbed all my body.

"I am burned. I'm finished." I began to cry.

"Let her go!"

"I will."

"Say that you have let her go!"

"Where should I go after I let her go?"

"Go to hell!"

"How can I go to hell?"

"That is where you belong."

He hit me with tuaf. The hot wax of the candle dripped on to my stomach as cotton threads of the candle swung against my body.

"Let her go now!"

"Okay, here I let her go!"

"Swear that you won't come back to her."

"How should I swear?"

"Swear that if you come back, and if you do, you will be slaughtered by the sword of Saint Michael."

"What if I don't keep my word and come back to her?"

"I told you if you do so, Saint Michael will cut off your body into pieces."

"I can't promise."

The priest hit me hard on my head. They poured more Holy Water on me.

"I won't return to her if she goes to Church."

"Say that if you do, you will be slaughtered by Saint Michael's sword."

"Let me be slaughtered with Michael's sword. I won't go near her if she goes to Church.

I then pretended that I fainted. And when I opened my eyes, I acted as if I knew nothing about what had been going on around. The priest said to me sympathetically, "It's okay. You'll be fine."

My father was silent for most of our walk home. When he finally spoke, regret filled his voice. "Emuye, you are innocent and trusting. This is wrong. At the church, there are genuine Christians, as well boys that came with an evil mission. I acted in fear, stopping you from church because I wanted to protect you. Now you need to protect yourself from these boys. I will not forbid you from going to church anymore."

I felt like ululating and kissing the ground for I was overjoyed. But I somehow managed to control my happiness and restrain myself from doing that.

After that day, it was my parents who reminded me to go to church. If I ever wanted to stay away from church because of bad weather, they would say, "This is a temptation from Satan. You do not have to stay long, go and come back quickly," and they forced me to go.

Chapter 4

Yeneta, a priest who taught at the spiritual school, was one of the priests who was present while the Holy Water was poured over me. He was my father's *nefs abate*, and so my father visited him often to confess his sins. He was also close friends with my father and came to our house often, so I was afraid that he might have seen through my act. I often met him on my way to church. He did not oppose my going to church, my spiritual devotion, or my being a devout Christian, but I sensed he was displeased about something. One day while I was at the church resting under the shade of a tree listening to the sweet songs of the students after I had prayed my personal prayer, Yeneta came up to me. I was surprised to see him and jumped to my feet. He was short—when I stood I was as tall as him. He greeted me and I bowed down to kiss the hand cross he carried in his right hand.

"The Holy Book says, 'Eteqewim nefs ze- enbela siga,'" he said. I recognized that he was quoting a biblical verse in Ge'ez, although I had not studied that language.

"What does it mean?" I asked.

"This is almost Amharic." He smiled.

"I know little Ge,ez. I did not study the language."

"It means, 'Soul cannot exist without flesh.'"

Here is my father, I thought.

I was not happy as he distracted me from listening to what I considered the sweet songs of angels. The spot in which I sat was not easily noticeable; and no one knew that I usually came here. Yeneta must have followed me after I had prayed. I did not try to hide my displeasure at being bothered.

"I am not here to disturb you. I just want to express my concern."

"Why are you concerned?" I asked.

"I am concerned because the soul cannot exist without the flesh."

What the hell is he talking about? I thought angrily.

He continued. "You can't depend on your parents forever. How do you plan to make ends meet in the future?"

"I have never thought about that."

"Are you thinking of becoming a nun?"

"I don't think so."

Looking into my eyes with his old eyes with grey rings around the iris, he said, "If so, until God calls you to heaven, you have to think about what you will do while you are living on this earth."

"Only God knows about that," I said hoping to cut the conversation short.

"Yes, you are right. But you also need to think about your future."

He held a hard cover book in a small leather bag hanging over his shoulder. He opened it flipped some pages. Handing me the book, he said, "Read this page."

It was Dirsane Michael, a book about the work and miracles done by Saint Michael.

He had opened it to Yekatit 12. The left page was in Geez and the right one translated in Amharic. Yeneta pointed at the Amharic page.

I began to read. "There was a man who was a devout Christian. He prayed day and night. He always asked Saint Michael, 'My Lord, feel pity for me. Give me food daily and cloth me once a year. But he was lazy and never went out of his house to work. He did not know any work. He did not even work for one hour a day. He did not also know to trade.

"Then, the Archangel Saint Michael came to the lazy poor man in his dream. He said to him, 'You lazy man, who don't like farming or trading, why do you beg me day and night to have mercy on you? In order for me to bless it where is your vine yard? Where is your wheat farm? Where is what you have produced? Where is what you have toiled away at?

"'You lazy man, where is what you sell or what you buy with? Why do you say, 'My Lord, Michael, feel pity for me.' Where is the work you toiled away at? Haven't you heard what God said to the father of all, Adam, when he sinned? You are from this land and you will go back to it. Didn't He say to him, 'Work and get your food with the sweat of your brow.' But you do not work, whereas you want me to bless you. He said this to him and went up to the sky...." I finished reading the page. The story intrigued me and I turned to the next page and continue reading when Yeneta stopped me.

He returned the book back nto the leather bag.

"So what did he have to be blessed?"

I kept quiet.

"The angel was right when he left him alone, wasn't he?" Yeneta asked.

I nodded.

He studied my face for few seconds and asked, "What do you and I have to be blessed?"

"You are a teacher," I answered.

He thought quietly for a while and said. "Okay, let's forget me. what about you?"

When I read the story, I felt that it was written about me. I knew Yeneta was going to ask this question.

I said, "I am a student. I am studying."

"Do all students who go to school become successful? Do all of them get employed?"

Yeneta asked this question because he knew a number of young people in our neighborhood who completed grade ten, even grade twelve, yet were unemployed.

"That is the will of God."

"God helps you when you work hard and ask for His help," he said adjusting the turban he wore.

I said nothing. I could hear the students singing. As if he wanted to listen to their song, Yeneta was quiet for several seconds.

"I teach these students God's word in the morning and evening. They know what I tell them is not enough; so they work hard to learn more, to understand and own the songs. They even want to know more and go to the woods to study. I think what you study in your school also needs to be studied. If you don't study, you will fail. It is when you study and do well in your education that you will be successful in life."

"When you live in this world, you need to be wise. You cannot be too pious and forget about your flesh. As long as you have not decided to become a nun, you have to think about your flesh. If you quit your spirituality and lead a mundane life, your soul will be hurt."

I thought about Yeneta's words. Was he trying to lead me away from God? He was highly respected and he had supported his point with Homily evidence by making me read the story from Dirssane Michael. If he had not made me read that story, I would have crossed my fingers thinking he was the Devil in the flesh of the priest.

My teacher Abeba had tried to advise me once, telling me not to spend a lot of time at the church or doing spiritual activities.

"Don't intervene in my spiritual life." I had replied angrily.

Surprised, she said, "No, I didn't mean to do that. I just want to tell you that you are not paying as much attention to your education as you should."

I had turned deaf ears to her advice. I regretted it now. I may need to apologize to her, I thought.

Chapter 5

After being allowed to go to Church, I became a kind and helpful girl. I was pleasant while I helped my mother with cooking, washing, and tidying the house so she would have less to do after she returned from her long days at work. I even went to the mill, tutored the minors, and did other household activities so that mother would not consider forbidding me from going to church.

Those things were easy, but following Yeneta's advice to focus on my studies was more difficult. I hated studying and reading. Whenever somebody gave me a book, especially a big one, I returned it without reading pretending that I had no time. I didn't even enjoy the books assigned by our Amharic teacher.

In spite of my love of God, I even loathed reading my father's Bible. For many years Yeneta had encouraged me to read Proverbs from the Bible. At first, I thought he invited me to study that book because he loved the son of King David, Solomon the Wise. Later, as he cited other carefully chosen chapters from the Bible, I suspected that Yeneta wanted me to get some message from the readings.

That afternoon after my discussion with Yeneta outside of the church, I just went home and opened the Bible and began reading Proverbs from one of the chapters that Yeneta had suggested.

"My son, go to the point of exhaustion. Allow no sleep to your eyes. Go to the ant, you sluggard; consider its ways and wise. How long you will lie there, you sluggard? When will you get up from your sleep...and poverty will come on you like a thief and scarcity like an armed man..."

I closed the book and sat speechless for some time. I was deeply touched by what I read. After a while I asked myself, "What am I? Am I the sluggard, the lost?" Harsher words rushed through my mind. Everything I read about the sluggish son described me well. This shocked me.

I remembered Teacher Abeba who had given me two books. "These are timeless and incredible books," she said while handing them over. She confided that they had changed her life for the better. At first, I thought she was boasting.

"I hope you liked the books," she said a few days later.

I told her that I had not read them.

"Please, read those books for me?" she pleaded. I began reading one of the books but could not finish it. I found it quite boring.

After my discussion with Yeneta and reading the Proverbs, I picked up Teacher Abeba's books again as I suspected that she too wanted to tell me something. I understood now that she must have had a purpose for giving me the books, otherwise, she could simply have given me a skirt or a pair of shoes for my errands. I decided to read both books.

The book I had not opened at all was entitled Anne Frank's Diary. Just before the preface, there was an inscription: "You know my eternal wish, Katy. I want to be a kind of woman who walks tall and see the world in the face, who knows where to go and determined to get there, and who never flinch for thunder or lightening ... what can I say... full-fledged woman.

"I can't imagine having to live like Mother, Mrs. van Daan and all the women who go about their work and are then forgotten. I need to have something besides a husband and children to devote myself to. I don't want to have lived in vain like most people. I want to be useful or bring enjoyment to all people, even those I've never met. I want to go on living even after my death! And that's why

I'm so grateful to God for having given me this gift, which I can use to develop myself and to express all that's inside me!"

"This is what Anne Frank tells you, Emebet. What is your plan Emu? What do you want to be?" I murmured. It was my first time raising such a question for myself. I have no talent, trade or anything to which to aspire. I was just another woman destined to spend a meaningless life at home."

I said to myself, "Poor Emu, do you want to spend your life this way?"

"No. Never," the other part of me responded.

"What shall I do?" I was confused.

I had no vision until the family, nefs abat, and Teacher Ababa forced me to read the Proverbs and Anne Frank's Diary respectively. I just ate, slept, and went to and from the school and church. Such a monotonous life!

I didn't know what to say if someone asked me about my future. I might have said "I want to be a doctor," in response to a teacher's request, but it would not be true. All I wanted was to remain faithful throughout my life, worshiping the almighty God. I was religious not only due to family pressure but also due a force within me. I already responded positively to this call. But I never thought about how I would manage to live an independent life.

I had never worried about my future before. It was not just because I was still young. It was something more. Had I been asleep for years? The priest and my teacher had tried to wake me often, but I had turned deaf ears to their advice. I had even ignored my mother when she cautioned me about my future.

I thought about one time when she spoke to me. She had been braiding my hair one Saturday. I always longed for Saturday to come for I couldn't wait my mother to braid my hair. There are no beauty salons in Ayehu. Some women braided hair at their home as a part time job, and many of my friends used their services, but my mother who washed and braided my hair. She did not let anyone braid my hair. I always felt so happy when I sat in between her thighs, she on a stool and me on a sheep's skin, while she gently combed my hair and told me different stories, advising me or confiding in me about her thoughts and feelings about different subjects. On the Saturday I remembered, before Yeneta talked to me about my education, I sat between her knees outside our house in the beautiful sunshine. Sossina was making *shiro wot,* while my sister and brother were playing volleyball with a ball made of rag a few yards away from where I sat with my mother.

"Emawayish." My mother called me the name she only used to express her love.

"Yes," I replied.

"What do you think of your future?"

"What?" I asked, surprised by the turn in the conversation.

"I saw some of the children of the village being hired as laborers in the commercial farm." She was referring to those children who failed to pass the Ethiopian School Leaving Certificate Examination and who couldn't continue athigher learning institutions after completion of grade twelve.

"Don't worry about me, mother," I replied.

"Why shouldn't I worry? Am I not your mother?"

"I know I can live better than the others."

"How can you be sure?"

I didn't know to be honest, but I could not imagine myself in misery. I kept quiet. Mother did not leave me alone, though. "If you really know you have a better future, why don't you show me the way?" she inquired.

I still kept silent.

"Tell me how I can improve my life. Am I not your mother? Don't you see that I am suffering from the terrible blows of life? I didn't know that you are such a cruel girl."

"What did I do to you, mother?"

"You are not willing to tell me."

"Tell you what?"

"Your miraculous way of improving one's life."

I did not respond. I did not know how to express my confidence that I would be okay even though I did not have a plan.

My mother did not say anything either. She finished braiding my hair, and then we washed our hands and went into the hut for lunch.

While we ate, mother resumed her line of questioning.

"Emawaye."

"Yes, mother." I said.

"Tell me now."

"What is there to tell you?"

"Your miraculous way of improving one's life."

I did not have an answer then. Hoping to divert her attention, I said, "You will choke. Don't talk while eating." She continued looking at me, expectantly, so I pleaded. "Can't you forget it?"

"No, I won't forget it!" she said holding the gursha, a lap of injera, she had rolled.

"Why do you seek a better life than you have?" I asked.

She turned to her left then to her right, surveying our house. I followed her gaze as she observed the cracked unpainted walls, rough floor, worn-out bedspread, and the earthen stage that we use as couch, a bench, and a bed.

"Are you telling me that this is life?" she said.

I kept silent.

Mother often compared her livelihood with the residents in the Building Block Site. The residential houses of the workers of the Commercial Farm had three levels. The first is Building Blocks Site. Homes located in this site are with one-bedroom made of bricks, concrete floors and painted walls. They also have iron roofs with ceilings. Residents of this site, who had better salaries, got access to electric power until eleven pm, and enjoyed bathrooms with pit latrines.

The second type of houses are called the D Mud Houses Site. The walls of the houses in this site are made of mud and straw. The floors of the houses are not concrete and the walls are not painted. In this site, homes have no bedrooms, bathrooms, or pit latrines. Residents defecate at boreholes dug in the backyards. The family lives in a single room. However, houses in this site get access to electric power.

Our house is located on the third site which is called the Thatch Site. Homes in this site thatched houses and are a bit more spacious than the D Mud Houses Site. We also have neither bathrooms nor pit latrines. We use home-made lamps as we have no access to electric power.

"If I was educated, I would live in Building Block Site," she said, her words intended to instill ambition within me.

Mother recalled how Father used to entertain her in the early days of their marriage. Later, when he did not treat her as well, Mother contemplated divorce. But because of her children and her inability to secure her own income, she could not afford to leave.

I knew that my mother worried that because I was not doing well in school that I would not complete my formal education and I would end up in an arranged marriage like she did, unable to leave if I needed. She tried to make me understand that uneducated girls had no options, to make me wise, capable, and skilled to compensate for the mistakes she made in her own life. Up until I seriously considered the readings provided to me by Yeneta and my Teacher Abeba, I had never understood.

That Saturday afternoon, as soon as we finished eating, my brother,Workeneh had come in with his report card. My mother looked at the report and her face became as red as a ripe tomato. The veins on her neck grew larger and she gnashed her teeth. This was how she reacted when she became furious.

"Why don't you begin training on loading and unloading bags?" she said.

"Are you insane, Mother?" he replied.

"Well, if you don't want that trade, then learn how to live with hunger."

"Why do you say such horrible things?" I cried, lest the awful words could hurt the boy's feeling.

"Does he have better chance?" she said earnestly. "He will be digging for the Commercial Farm or be an errand boy unless he improves his grades. There is no other option. So, he should acquaint himself with these trades sooner. There is no substitute for experience," she replied.

Father had returned from work and was lying on the bed and listening to our conversation. "Aster is right. These exam results will not take you anywhere. If you want to fill only your belly, be an errand boy. Otherwise, you should acquaint yourself with hunger."

Our parents were so unhappy about how my brother and I were performing at school. They refused to buy us new clothes. Instead, we were forced to wear used clothes. Whenever we asked for new clothes, our parents would say:

"Why should we buy you new clothes if you are not to wear such clothes in the future?"

"Why do you say so?"

"You won't have money to buy new clothes."

"I can work."

"What kind of work can you get with your educational status? Loading and unloading, being a runner, or working as house servant?"

Our parents had continued to tell us that we are waiting for gloomy future, but I did not listen until Yeneta enlightened me.

* * *

I sat in our hut reading on the books Abeba had given me. Although the sky was clear, the weather was cold in the hut. My mother said to me, "Emebet, you should do something about this cold."

I built a big warm fire. When much of the smoke was gone, we gathered around the fire. My father did not want to enjoy the comfort of the fire for he did not want to be spoiled so he stayed away from it bundled in his thick wool coat given to him for his work, covering his head with a warm shawl. My parents had both received salary raises. Their raises were unprecedentedly high; the farm took into consideration the existing inflation.

"How much salary increment have you got?" Mother asked Father.

"As the saying goes, the cat said, 'Even if a thousand cows are milked, I am given milk as much as the broken pot could hold.' Not much." He seemed sorry.

I had heard that for those positions that did not require much education, the incremental raises tended to be small. I was always ashamed when people asked me what my father did. My father was athletic and handsome. If it had been with physical beauty that higher salary was paid, he would have been one of the highly paid employees.

"Father, what made you choose guarding for a job?" I asked.

My father acted as if he had not heard my question.

"Why did you want to become a security guard?" I repeated louder.

"Uneducated man has no choice."

"Why didn't you go to school, Father?" I asked him a question I always had wanted to ask him.

"I had no one to support me."

"You could have learnt while helping yourself."

"Easier said than done."

"Ok, forget education. How come you didn't try to be a businessman?"

"You can't start up a business with no money," he said irritably. "What is the matter with you? Why don't you leave me alone?" He was deeply hurt by the dialogue.

This discussion really made me think about my situation and I finally realized that my fate would not be different from my parents unless I whole-heartedly pursued my education. Father, uneducated and living with meager salary, was very much worried about his future after his retirement. He was not sure whether he can educate his children or not. He should have prepared for his future and for ours but it was too late.

I began worrying about my future. I didn't want to lead a miserable life, and, more than anything, I don't want God to name me "You sluggish girl!" Instead, I wanted to help my parents and the needy. I decided to focus on school, got a good education, and grew up to have a respectable trade.

I read the two books, Anne Frank's Diary and You Can Win line by line. I loved the books. They offered me ideas that would help me attain my goal.

Chapter 6

I decided first of all to improve my skills in English language. Hence, I collected the right books for this purpose, and then I read them day and night in order to master the language well. I saved a new English word everyday recalling that one of our teachers said "A drop of water will make an ocean through time."

One day, after spending the whole day reading my books and notebooks, I walked toward the Gumri River in the early evening to relax. I strolled towards the stream appreciating the magnificence of the world around me. I observed the water was crystal clear upstream but got muddy as it flowed down a sloping land. It became pure again in the flatland. Where the land is flat, the river flows silently, unimpeded by rock outcroppings. I didn't know where it ended but it peacefully flowed as far as my eyes could see.

It seemed that the river left its trouble in the sloppy areas and became cleaner and cleaner in the flatland to enable local residents utilize it for different purposes. I compared this phenomenon with my life. Just like the troubled life in the beginning and the end.

The sky in the west was purple. The sun had already given warning that it was leaving the sky for the next actor. I started jogging towards my home so I would arrive before dark. My heart beat faster and faster.

I came across two women who were from our neighborhood. They were carrying piles of firewood on their backs. They were surprised to see me there, and they said, "What are you doing here alone?"

"I am just taking a walk," I said, smiling. They did not believe me. They scanned the surroundings suspecting that I was with someone else.

"This is crazy!" one of them muttered.

"Why are you surprised?" I asked them.

"There are alligators in the river. They could eat you."

One of them came closer to me. "There is another danger. Look at you! You are a young beautiful girl with budding breasts, cascading hair, towering height, and a pretty face. Your alluring body could also call for danger," she said pointing at my body parts as she mentioned them one by one.

I did not look like a girl from a poor family. I often attracted the eyes of not only boys of my age but also adult men. People said I resembled my mother. My mother was a beauty with brown complexion. She had beautiful dark eyes with thick and long eyelashes. She also had dark eyebrows. She had wonderful white teeth with a beautiful smile. Her thick long hair, which covered her shoulders, was alien to any hair oil except butter. She took good care of it.

I inherited my height from my father. I was much taller than my mother. No girl in my class was taller than me. I also looked older than most of them. I had heard people say that beauty was prerequisite for wealth and success. But for me beauty is a hurdle. My beauty made my life more difficult.

Chapter 7

O ne day, while father was off-duty, he and I walked on the road that took us to Ayehu River leaving behind the village called Sar Sefer. I did not know why my father invited me to walk on this road. There was nothing attractive along this way. The vast fields of corn had dried up and the land no longer had the beautiful deep green color. No Columbus monkey jumped from tree to tree, because there was not a single tree as far as the eye could see. The land was yellow, covered with the dried corn. The trees had been cut because when rain water dripped down the tree canopy, seeds could not germinate and grow. We were not far from our neighborhood but I was already tired. I was about to say to him, "Let's turn back," when he said, "Let's rest here for a while." And so, we sat by the side of the road, close to the corn farm. I could see smoke coming out of the thatch roofed huts from afar, and I imagined wives making coffee for their husbands.

We began discussing my future. "Emebetye," he said affectionately. I wondered why he was in such a good mood. I had not done anything extraordinary that day, I had just washed his clothes and polished his shoes. These things could not bring such attention, for sure.

"Emebetye" he said again.

"Yes, Father."

"Can I ask you something, if you don't mind?"

"Sure, go ahead." Why should I mind? I got more confused.

"I don't like the look of the young men in your Sunday School."

I kept silent. I did not like the direction of the discussion and it occurred to me that talking to me about church was the reason we were walking together. He had taken me out to speak to me privately so that my siblings wouldn't hear.

"Have they said anything to you?" he continued.

"What can they say?"

"I heard that some of them are going to the school just to be around the girls."

"I know nothing about it," I said truthfully.

"Don't make it secret. I am asking you lest they would hurt you in some way."

"Don't worry, Father. No one is interested in such things. Everyone is committed to his faith."

"Are you telling me you have not been with any of the boys?"

"Jesus Christ! What happened to you today?" I screamed. I felt sad that he suspected me of committing a sin.

"I won't be angry with you. Don't deny it." He added.

"No!"

"Can you swear about it?"

"Sure. In the name of the Holy Savior I didn't do such thing!"

"Bravo my darling! I know you will never humiliate me," he said.

It troubled me. Why is he so concerned about my virginity? What makes him raise the topic in the first place? Grapevine? Mother's warnings?

"I just told him that I am sure of your purity."

"To whom are you referring?"

"Aychew."

Aychew was a grain merchant living in Ayehu who owns a warehouse in the vicinity of the town. He bought pepper, teff, and maize in winter and traded the grains in summer with a profit.

"Did Aychew tell you that I made love to somebody?" I jumped to my feet and shouted, "He is a big liar!"

"Take it easy." He tugged at my skirt and made me sit down again.

I covered my ears with my palms and said, "I don't want to hear this."

He tapped my shoulder affectionately and said, "He said no such thing."

"Then why did he have to ask you about me?" I pushed his hand away from my shoulder.

I stood. He got to his feet and we continued our walk home.

"I think he is concerned about you."

"Concerned for me?" I was confused.

"Yes."

"What are you talking about, Father?" I didn't understand why he was so hesitant about telling me what was on his mind.

"Someone asked for your hand. You are going to marry."

"I don't want get married."

He continued talking, ignoring my protest. "You are fortunate, Aychew is very wealthy. He has two trucks, two houses in Bahir Dar and Dangila towns. I would beg to be his relation."

Early marriage is still practiced in North Western Ethiopia, particularly in Gojjam and Gondar. Marriages for younger children are usually arranged by the parents of the boy and the girl. Often such families are friends or close neighbors. I had heard of cases when such proposals were made while the child was still in the womb. While the wife of one family was pregnant another would say, "If the baby is a girl, she will be my son's wife." In Ayehu market, it is easy to spot teenagers that are thirteen and fourteen tying their waist with mekenet, a scarf, often colorful, made exclusively to be tied on the waist of married women. Girls could be married at the age of nine, but the parents of the boy promise not to let her husband, who was usually a few years older, not to have sexual relations with her until she was thirteen. But such promises are not always kept causing physical and psychological problems for the young girls. The government has introduced a law that bans marriage before eighteen years of age. But a number of early marriages are arranged secretly.

Now that my father had revealed Aychew's intentions, I understood why he had asked me about the boys in the Sunday School. I knew that Aychew wanted to marry me because I was a virgin. The spread of HIV in Ayehu area had led to men preferring to marry younger girls who had had no sexual experience. Single men preferred to marry a girl below sixteen years of age. Parents who were not sure of their daughter's integrity did not hesitate to give them away to single men in a bid to protect their girls from the incurable disease. Aychew probably wanted me, despite my age, because he was concerned about contracting HIV/AIDS.

I recognized that I was an attractive girl and that my being spiritual had enhanced my beauty, so I was expecting someone would propose to me sooner or later. Father was always anxious that someone would infect me with HIV virus. He was worried about my future. Moreover, the wealth of the businessman tempted him.

"He also has a great personality," my father continued.

"He may have everything in the world. But I don't want to marry right now."

"Are you telling me you don't know Aychew?"

"I didn't say so."

"Why won't you have him as a husband?"

"First, he is too old. Second, I shall finish my education first."

"Do you think Aychew is aged?"

"He must be at least thirty years old."

"A man should be a bit older than his wife."

"Are you telling me to marry a man sixteen years older than me?"

"Then, what kind of man do you want to marry?"

"I don't want to marry right now. He must be a man of my age if I want to."

"My daughter won't marry a boy!"

"What does that mean?"

"You shall marry an independent and responsible adult not a youngster."

"I don't want to marry now, anyway."

We arrived home. When I was about to enter into our hut, he held my hand, "Think it over," he said with a low voice.

"I don't need any more time to think about this," I murmured and went in leaving him outside.

He seemed to forget the issue for days and began persuading me to marry the man again. We were at home while my siblings were at school and Mother had not returned from work.

"What vices does Aychew have?"

"I did not say he has any." I did not want to complain about his age again.

"If so, why don't you marry him?"

"Think about my education."

"He promised to send you to school."

"He may change his mind."

"What does it matter if you drop out of school?"

"For what sake?"

"As I can see, education will not help you earn your livelihood."

I wanted to tell him that he is a pessimist but refrained because I did not want to insult his fatherhood.

"Do you dream about my fate? Did God tell you so?" I was very much depressed.

"I saw no dream," he said.

"How do you know education is not for me then?"

"You can tell a scholar when you see one."

"I was careless about education before. But from today onwards..."

"Do you think you can alter luck? 'A gram of chance is greater than a ton of knowledge.'"

"I don't agree with this. God ordered Adam and Eve to live by the sweat of their brows."

"But you have been suffering from your lessons just to pass from one grade level to the next one let alone to join a university."

"The Almighty God is with me!" I never expected such a discouraging talk from my father. I felt so low. "I have become a burden, right?"

"I didn't say."

"You worry too much about my education."

"I didn't say so."

"You are forcing me to marry somebody I didn't love."

"Because I want you to live a good life."

"Do you think no one would marry me when I get a bit older until completing my education?"

"Aychew will not wait for you that long."

"I don't care. He is not the only man in the world"

"Marrying Aychew is equivalent to winning a lottery."

"God will get someone for me."

"I prefer you to marry Aychew to any other man."

"Why?"

"He is prosperous. You would have a happy life. It would be good for us. Especially, it would be fine for your sisters and brothers. We, the parents, won't bother you much. We can live with my retirement."

"Wait for me until I complete my education, then I will support all of you."

"When?"

"May be in twelve years."

"The grass would cover my grave by then."

"You won't die so soon."

"Forget about me, how about the fate of your sisters?"

"Just live the way you live now."

"This is a curse."

"No."

"You just want us to live this way for the coming years."

"And what if Aychew refuses to help you after the marriage?"

"He won't if really loves you."

"Money may change him, you know. He may even hate me after some time. Men are deceptive. What can I do if he wants to divorce me after a while? Can I force him to stay with me as a husband? Am I to sue him for sharing his own wealth with me? It would be better if I made my own fortune and assisted you after completing my education."

"You are throwing away your best chance."

"Don't worry, I will find better."

"Good luck never visits a person twice!"

"An untimely marriage is an obstacle for girls' success rather than a fortune."

"You are foolish," he grieved.

"I am just fourteen years old. I shall not marry at this time of my age," I told him firmly.

"I thought you love and respect me."

"I do."

"You would do what I wanted you to do if you loved me."

"I can't marry anyone right now!"

Chapter 8

The next day when mother and I returned from church, we sat to take our breakfast. Sossina had prepared a tasty breakfast, a delicious *firfir*, broken *injera* rinsed in spicy soup. She was becoming a good cook. I was starving and had a big appetite. Mother and I were alone. Father was at work and Sossina had left after preparing the food.

Mother took a glimpse at me and said, "Why did you go to sleep without eating your dinner last night?"

"I was angry."

"With whom were you angry? With your father?"

"Yes, who else?" I said remembering the words of my father.

"What did happened this time?" my mother asked. She knew we had not been fighting since I began to pay more attention to my education.

"Didn't he tell you his plan for my future life?"

"No, he didn't."

I was surprised to hear that.

"He wants me to marry Aychew."

"What?" She had been about to put some food in her mouth but she returned the food to the tray.

I did not stop eating.

Mother dropped her head and held her forehead with her hand. She was visibly sad. I felt relieved to find that my mother was on my side.

"Please eat," I told her.

"I'm full," she said.

"He did not only want me to marry."

"What else?"

"He said I would achieve nothing by going to school."

"Yes, this is annoying."

I was happy that my mother was able to feel the same resentment I did.

After having breakfast, while drinking tea, I asked mother, "What do you advise me?" I was worried about my father's rigidity.

"It is your life. It is up to you to make the decision."

"I know, but I want your motherly advice."

She thought quietly for some minutes.

"Your father is not good to me."

"I know," I said nodding and encouraging her to tell me more.

"He despises me and cares little about me. I lived all these years with him because I wanted to raise you. Because I don't have the means to raise you. I am disappointed in my parents. They should have helped me continue my education. I could have become at least an elementary school teacher if I had completed high school. Your father despises me because he knew I have nowhere to go. When you are financially dependent on your husband, you have little influence and power even at your home. Your husband can mistreat you. You can be successful in your education if you continue to give the attention you are giving to it now. I don't advise you to get married before you are on your way to becoming self-reliant. ."

"I would rather not marry."

"I don't want to intervene. If I get involved it will anger your father and he may force you to marry Aychew. You make your decision. You know what you should do."

* * *

I was daydreaming. Sometimes I dreamed of joining a university, wearing a white overcoat while I helped patients in the hospital, or waiting for customers with my office door wide open. In my dream, people praise me saying my mother ought to have born lots of twins just like me. I felt the seed of an important person growing within me like tree and shading creatures suffering from the drought of a desert. My dream motivated me even further and I read longer hours every day.

Father, on the contrary, seemed determined to kill my dream. Four days after we discussed about the marriage, I was on my way home from school and I met with my two sisters and brother who were on their way to the afternoon shift of school. I asked Sossina for the key to the house.

"It's not locked. Father is there," she said.

When I entered the house, I saw father sleeping on his bed. Moving quietly, I ate my lunch and began studying.

When he woke up, I said to him, "Do you want to have lunch?"

"I have had lunch," he answered. "What are you doing?" he asked after a while.

"I'm studying," I said taking a glimpse at him.

"You're just wasting your time," he said putting the pillow against the wall and leaning on it.

"You think I will not be successful in my studies?" I stared at him.

"Do you doubt that? You're doomed to fail," he replied staring back at me.

"Don't say that to me!" I said feeling anger welling up within me.

"I don't think you would pass to grade eleven let alone joining university."

"As a father you should be encouraging me. I don't expect this from you."

"Face the reality! You'll see."

Go to hell! I silently said to myself feeling miserable. "Are you a prophet to say that?"

"I don't need to be a prophet. Just look at yourself! You have no good foundation. You wasted too much time at the church. Now it is too late. A tree has to grow from a seed to finally become a big tree. Everything has its own foundation. You cannot dream about university when you have no strong foundation in your education."

"Father don't forget what you just said. Jot it down on your notebook if you like."

"I won't waste a single minute doing that," he replied.

I kept quiet.

I could not stop thinking about our conversation afterwards. I hated him for saying those words and I feared he would force me to marry Aychew. I did not want to stay at home that night. I left for Abeba's house leaving a note to my mother not to expect me to come that evening.

I knocked on the door and pushed it to get into the room. My Teacher Abeba looked up. Her face brightened with a smile. She stood, walked towards me, and hugged me. I sat next to her on a stool. She was correcting exam papers.

"Can I help you with anything?" I said.

"Yes, I have not cooked *wot*."

She lived in a one room house divided into two by a curtain. Hidden behind the curtain were the cooking utensils and dishes. Her bed was covered by a quilt decorated with knitted flowers but otherwise her house was sparsely decorated. Mud was visible where the whitewash had flaked off of the walls. Teacher Abeba had once told me that she had not done much to improve on the house as she had no plan to stay long in Ayehu.

I used the kerosene stove and made shiro wot. I then read my exercise books.

It got dark and Abeba lit a kerosene lamp. When she finished her work, she glanced at her watch and was surprised to see that it was 10:00 PM in the evening. I never stayed this late.

"Oh sorry, I made you stay long," she said.

"I would like to sleep here."

"Have you let your parents know?"

"Yes, I left a note for my mother."

"It's okay then. You know I like your company," she said and smiled.

After eating our dinner, Abeba gently said, "You are not alright these days. Is something wrong?"

"Yes, you're right. There is a problem."

"What is it?"

"My father wants me to get married."

I remembered my confrontation with my father that afternoon, and the cruelty with which he told me that I would achieve nothing in my education. Tears filled my eyes.

"Take it easy. You don't have to cry."

I felt sad and helpless. I burst into tears.

Abeba comforted me. "He can't force you to marry," she said wiping my tears from my cheeks.

"He is forcing me. I am thinking about fleeing to Bahir Dar or Addis Ababa."

"That might be worse."

"Someone may hire me as a housemaid. I can learn in the evening education program while working."

"That is risky, too. You may get an employer who abuses you."

"What shall I do then? Father will never leave me alone unless I am out of his sight."

"Don't worry. I am with you."

I relaxed a little, comforted by her support.

Chapter 9

For the next few days, I lived with Abeba, only going home when I knew my father was absent to help my family with the household work. I also went to church. My parents did not come looking for me.

Living with Abeba was a great opportunity. I was free from my father's nagging, but I was not free living with Abeba. I felt like an intruder and a burden to her.

One day she said to me, "I will talk to your father and will look for lasting solution."

I personally did not expect that Abeba would make my father change his mind about my marriage. .

About five days after I came to Abeba, I was coming back from church with Senait.

"Have you observed the great gift of singing Kassa and Gizaw have?" I said to her.

She didn't answer.

I went on speaking, "They are both talented. But Kassa is better when he plays the drum."

"Have you done well in your English exam?" Senait asked. I felt that she wanted to change the subject, but I didn't know why.

"It was good. .... Have you heard Gizaw singing? Even the birds seem to enjoy his..."

She changed the subject but I remained admanant.

"Eh, once you start talking about something, you never get tired of it," she snapped.

"What happened to you? Do they bore you?"

"I don't like them. They are phoney." She seemed almost depressed at the mention of their names.

"What is phoney about them?"

"They come to church just to see the girls."

"I don't believe this. Why are you tarnishing their names?"

"Just wait and see."

I was angry at what Senait suggested because those boys were my role models with respect to spiritual life.

Of course, gossip circulated around what the Sunday School boys and girls like, "They turned the forest into bedrooms" and "Those boys are ruining the church." But I had never seen anything for myself and the boys had always been respectful towards me. I did not believe the rumors were true.

Surprisingly, within the same week my mother's friend said, "Don't trust Gizaw and Kassa," and told me about their wicked behaviour in detail.

"No, they are not such bad boys," I objected.

"Let God safeguard you for the sake of your innocence."

I began paying attention to what people were saying about the two boys. There was so much gossip I began to think that some of it might be true. I stopped going to church for a while to avoid meeting the boys and also to prepare for the eighth grade examination.

* * *

My teacher Abeba reconciled me with my father and I returned home. Although my father no longer spoke about my getting married, I avoided him as much as possible by staying at school.

In the first week of my return home, I was on the morning shift that week and my siblings were on the afternoon shift. That Wednesday, my father was at work, my mother had not returned from work yet. I was studying sitting on the *medeb* when I heard someone at the door. They were Kassa and Gizaw. I looked behind them to see if Yared was with them as they were often together, but they were alone. I was not happy that they came to my home. Because of their bad reputations, my parents would not be happy to hear that they had been around. My father had warned me not to be seen hanging around boys. Once he showed me two bullets; and pointing at me with one of them he said, "This is for you;" and with the other to himself and said, "and this is for me, if you cause any shame to me."

Since there was no one in the house except the boys and me, it would be a top talking point for gossipers.

"Emebet, my love, we have missed you at church," said Kassa.

"Please don't call me that," I said feeling embarrassed.

"What is wrong with it?"

"It makes you sound as if you were my lover."

"Do you think I don't love you?"

"If you loved me, you would leave. My father has warned me not to be seen with boys anywhere. He detests the idea of my having an affair with boys at the church.

He has beaten me for going to church before and lets me go to church only because he doesn't want me to fall ill. If he sees or hears that boys are here looking for me, you can imagine what will happen to me."

I went to the door and looked around.

"You're being tempted by the devil."

"It could be. But I don't blame my father. He is the father of a daughter. And you know that the news about Tirngo is still fresh in the minds of many."

"But we are spiritual people," Kassa said.

Gizaw nodded.

"I hope you don't mind if I tell you that many people consider you to be bad boys."

"We don't care. God knows who we are."

"The problem is for us, the girls. My return to the Sunday School is a special case. There are several girls who are not still allowed to go. Once some bad news is attached to a girl, her whole life would be spoiled by it."

"So you don't want to be with us?" Kassa said, disappointed.

"I hope you'll understand my problem." I continued, "If your intention is serving God limit your relationship with the girls. If you do so, people will trust you and listen to the words of God that you tell them."

"I don't think we are the source of your problem. Your parents are too strict. We heard that they kicked you out and were at your teacher's house for a few days," Gizaw said.

I was not surprised that they heard for Ayehu was too small for such big news not to be heard.

"You don't know what is going to happen tomorrow. Why don't you declare your freedom?" Kassa added.

"Declare my freedom?"

'Oh yes, for how long do you have to live like this?"

I folded my hands over my chest and looked at him as if he were foolish, "Are you kidding? How can a fourteen year old girl declare her freedom?"

"We mean it."

I went to the door again to check if my mother came. The road was clear.

"Sorry, my mother will be here soon. Please go!"

Glancing at his wrist watch Gizaw said, "It's now four thirty in the afternoon."

"She doesn't wait until five o'clock. If she is done with her work, she will come."

"Okay let's come to the point. You know how you declare your freedom?"

"How do I declare my freedom?"

"You can marry, you know."

I chuckled and snapped, "Go to hell!"

"I mean it. Get married, declare your freedom from your parents, and do what you feel is good," Kassa said.

"In the name of God, thanks for your advice."

"In fact our call today was not only to persuade you to come to the congregation but also to encourage you to get married."

"How very thoughtful of you!"

"Emuye, please don't joke about this."

"I won't." Now I understand the gossip about them was not for nothing.

"Please tell us the fact."

"What fact?"

"What shall we say to the person who sent us to you?"

"Who sent you here?"

"We are forbidden to mention his name unless you agree with his proposal."

"I won't say anything until you tell me who he is."

"Emuye! You should believe us! He is a very good man. He is handsome; humble....He is flawless."

"If he is as perfect as you have described, get him another wife."

"You are his choice."

"I am not willing to marry for now."

"Do you wish him to send elders to your parents?"

"No. It won't make me change my stand."

They didn't care a bit about my fear. I was nervous that my mother would get home before they leave. My mother could also get the information from someone. What a challenge!

"Enjoy yourselves!" I snapped and went out.

I was going to Senait's house.

Following behind me Gizaw shouted, "Wait! ...Wait!"

I shut him up and walked quickly.

He ran after me and held my hand. I snatched my hand away from his. "Leave me alone!"

"We'll come back tomorrow," he said and when I did not respond he added, "Did you hear me?"

Chapter 10

After Kassa and Gizaw left, I could not help wondering which of the boys had made this proposal of marriage. I thought about each of the boys who came to the Sunday School. None of them had ever approached me or showed special interest in me.

The only boys I spoke to were Gizaw, Kassa, and Yared, and with them I only have ordinary conversations. Gizaw, who was my classmate in eighth grade, lived with his uncle. He was still in school and couldn't possibly be thinking of marrying and adding another burden to his uncle.

Kassa was older than all of us. He had failed the ESLCE after completing grade twelve and worked as a daily labourer in the Commercial Farm. Yared also worked for the Commercial Farm. He had dropped out from school in the ninth grade to assist his disabled mother, his brothers, and a sister. Neither of these boys earns more than 120 Ethiopian Birr a month and they could not be considering marrying me with a chicken-feed salary.

I asked one of my classmates from the Sunday School. "Do you know which boy wants to marry me?"

"You will be told only when you agree to marry him," the girl replied.

"This is weird. How can I accept a proposal before knowing who he is? What if he is a rogue?"

"He is not."

"Who is he, then?"

"Promise to marry him."

"Impossible!"

"Hence, it is better if you never know who he is." She refused to disclose the identity of the boy.

"It won't be a secret for a long," I said disappointed.

Poverty could not hide my beauty. We did not eat good food, but still I was tall and good looking. My friends envied of my beauty. They particularly were often jealous of my long hair. "How lucky you are!" they said. I heard that beauty was an asset. But I did not agree. My beauty was an obstacle to my education and my goals. I was only fourteen and, two men had proposed to me. I was not sure what will happen tomorrow or the day after.

I did not know how many proposals I might get until I complete high school. It would have been better if I was not beautiful. I always wished I had a bright mind instead of a pretty face.

Afew weeks later, Yared's mother fell ill and my mother sent me to her to bake *injera* for the family. The bed-ridden mother looked pale. She had lost a lot of weight. It seemed her days were numbered. In spite of that, her voice was full of energy.

Their claypan was in bad shape and it was an agony to bake *injera* with such a pan. It was rough with many cracks in it. I filled the cracks with roasted and ground mustard seed so that the thin *teff* flour dough did not fall into the cracks when I bake the *injera*. The pan became smooth when I rubbed it with the ground mustard seed and it became easy to pick the hot *injera* once the claypan was rubbed well.

"Show me your injera," said the bed-ridden mother. I gave her a piece of *injera* coated with a peppered sauce. After keenly observing it, she said "It is good, great!" and murmured something to herself while gazing at the ceiling.

"What are you saying, mother?"

"I am blessing God."

"You are blessing God just because I helped you?"

"Not only for your assistance, dear."

"Then, it must be for you getting better."

"I wouldn't have bothered you if I was really better..."

"What is there to thank God for, then?"

"My son is to have a wife who is a good cook."

I knew she must be talking about Yared as he is the only one in the family at the right age for marriage.

"Is it Yared who is to marry someone?"

"Yes. It is him."

"Who is the bride?"

"It is you."

I stood speechless.

I know Yared, Gizaw, and Kassa are best friends. They are always together. I had been surprised that Yared never called on me with the two boys. Now I know why. Yared's home was nearer to our home than the two other boys. Yared's parents were closer to my parents. Although our families have no blood-relations, they act as if they do.

While I was preparing to leave I said, "I wish you a quick recovery, mother."

"Wait for a while," she said. "We shall have lunch together."

"I'm not hungry."

"It is just lunch-time."

"I had my breakfast very recently," I replied. I was eager to leave the house.

"I would be happy if you would have lunch with me."

"I am really not hungry."

"Fine, come closer."

I obeyed.

"Let me see your palm."

I agreed. She spat on my palm and earnestly blessed me. "Let you be above your peers! Be wealthy! Bear many children! Let your children be blessed."

All of this for assisting her for a day! It must be more than that! Is she really aspiring to make me her daughter-in-law? I felt sorry for her. It was better for Yared and me to be brother and sister.

Though I didn't like what Yared's mother wanted, I didn't want to abandon her. She was in a difficult condition and there was no one to care for her. I continued serving her as long as I could, although people talked a lot about it, speculating that I helped her because I planned to marry her son.

Chapter 11

O ne day after school, I was on my way into the church when two priests called me. First, I crossed myself with the Holy Cross and politely saluted them as usual.

"We shall pray before the discussion," the older priest, who was a monk and the head of the priests, suggested and so we prayed. The faithful began coming into the church to pray around five pm. The priest said, "Let's find a private place. We shall not be disturbed during our discussion." The younger priest and I obeyed.

The monk took out his cross and said, "My daughter, listen to me carefully, we called you to talk you about an important issue. No one shall hear this except your parents."

"What is the matter, father?"

"Yared beseeched us to ask you for marriage."

"Oh!" I was surprised that Yared had made a formal proposal without speaking to me or my parents.

"We understand that you know Yared better than we do," the priest began. "Do you know something bad about the boy?"

"No. But I don't want to marry right now."

"Why not?"

"I want to complete my education first..."

"He promised to send you to school after..."

"How can he do that?"

I knew he couldn't even afford to go to school himself, let alone educating me. His father had passed away long ago. His mother was always sick and a poor housewife. Two of his bothers and his sister were either students or too young to get employed. He is an electrician, but his wage is not better than a daily labourer.

Though the family receives one hundred and fifty Birr monthly from their father's retirement, they led a miserable life. They earned a monthly income of just three hundred Birr for a five-member family. How can I agree to be the sixth member of such a family? I felt the burden of his family's poverty bending my back.

"You don't know what God will do for Yared," the priest said. "Maybe God will grant him with an enormous wealth."

"That may happen. But I want to assist my humble family after completing my education. I don't plan to marry now."

"Education is not meant for you," said the young priest.

I wanted to tell him that he is a pessimist, that I was smart and I would succeed, but I swallowed it all and instead I said, "You dreamt about it? Are you telling me God revealed this for you?"

"I saw no such thing."

I was about to say to him, "If God did not reveal it to you, you must have gone to a fortune teller." But I can't say so for a priest, "How do you know education is not meant for me then?"

"Your father said you are not doing well in your education."

"May be I have not been able to score high grades so far. But I am working hard and from now onwards..."

"Do you think only hard work matters for one's success?"

It was my first time to hear such a discouraging remark from a priest. He annoyed me. I, however, had no other alternative except to stifle my fury.

"With the help of God, anything is possible!"

After thinking for a while, the older priest said, "We will not force you to agree. But you shall think about it."

I thought the matter was settled once and for all. I was wrong again.

A fortnight later, the older priest approached me again outside of the church. "What is your decision?"

"I still don't want to marry."

"You still don't need to get married?"

"That is right, father," I said dropping my eyes to the ground.

The church did not let couples to get married unless it confirmed that the girl agreed to marry the man. And so the head priest of the church said to me, "We don't force you unless you agree to get married." I felt relived hoping that Yared wouldn't bother me anymore.

But the younger priest who was with him the other day couldn't leave me alone. He called me one day and said; "Hold this Holy Cross!"

"Why?"

"Do you believe in the Holy Cross?" he inquired.

"I do."

"Then, hold it tight."

I did.

"I want you to swear to God so that you will obey me."
I released the cross in shock.

"Don't push me to the limit, Father!"

"You don't believe in the Holy Cross," he said.

"I do. But I won't swear to obey you when I don't know
your intentions."

"Will you become a nun? Are you not getting married at
all?"

"I haven't thought about it yet."

"When will you decide whether you will become a nun
or not?"

"I will decide after I have achieved my goal in life."

"You don't respect me." He looked offended.

"Of course, I do respect you. But..." I left him right
there. I didn't care if he thought I was disrespectful. He
has nothing to do with my future!

Chapter 12

After I left the priest, I headed home. I saw a group of baboons when I got close to Gumri River. I changed my direction and took another road because I had heard that baboons attack women, particularly girls. Soon I heard someone calling my name. I turned around to see Kassa. I was not happy to see him but I waited for him. We chatted on our way.

"How did you respond when Yared proposed to you?" Kassa wanted to know.

Kassa and Gizaw already knew that Yared had sent the priests to me although they did not know my response which was a surprise.

"... I said no because I don't want to marry anyone now and ..."

"You did well!"

I could see that he was happy. I was surprised. "Didn't you nag me to marry him before?"

"I was wrong. You should never marry him."

I decided to tease Kassa a little. "I am going to marry him. I said 'yes' to the priests."

"That is insane!" He looked truly shocked.

"Really?" I wondered what Kassa had in mind now.

"Life will be challenging for you. How can he lead a six-member family with less than three hundred Birr monthly income? Think about it! You would bear children. He can only buy the cheapest perfume for three hundred Birr and sprinkle it over the family."

I laughed.

"What makes you laugh?"

"The way you expressed the situation he is in."

"My intention was not to make you laugh." He was serious.

"It is funny, though." I said laughing.

"What surprised me most is that he promised to send you to school," said Kassa.

"What is so funny about it?"

"It is funny indeed. Do you think three hundred Birr can do everything?" He held up three of his fingers. "He is even planning to send you to town, rent a house, provisions, and then educate you with only three hundred Birr salary. There is no cost for such wishful thinking.'"

"You told me he is to be a permanent employee, remember?" I asked feeling ashamed for Kassa. He was betraying his friend without feeling a bit guilty.

"It is a hope that may not be realized," he replied.

Just weeks earlier, he was the one who was nagging me to marry Yared. Now he was pleased that I refused to his friend's proposal. I needed to know what was behind his sudden change of heart. He made it clear quite quickly.

"By the way, you know I have no family to support. My income is only for me."

"I know."

"Will you marry me, please?" He stared at me beseechingly.

"What?" I couldn't believe my ears. "You are kidding, right?"

"No."

"May be you are putting me to a test," I said laughing.

"I am damn serious." He knitted his brows.

"Can you swear in the name of St. Mary?"

"In the name of St. Mary and the St. Michael, I want to marry you right now"

"You are a deceitful." I was annoyed. "Yared sent you as a friend and you betray him! Get out of here!" I shouted at him.

He shrank back, shocked by my response. He then said with a trembling voice, "You refused to accept his proposal, didn't you?"

"You would try even if I had agreed! You are horrible..."

Chapter 13

When he lost hope in the assistance of the priests and his so-called "friends", Yared began approaching me himself. One day, on my way home from school, I saw him standing by the side of the road. I stood and waited for him.

He roared, "Why do you reject me? Am I too short? Too thin?"

"You are being provocative. Don't irritate me."

"Just answer me."

"I just want to focus on my education."

"Didn't they tell you that I agreed to send you to school?" He was visibly offended.

"They did tell me. I just want to learn independently."

"What if you go to school after you got married?"

"Education would be difficult after marriage. You know I will have a lot of responsibilities being a married woman

and I won't be able to focus on my studies. I am so sorry."
We walked silently for some distance.

"By the way, why do you want to get married soon?
What does having a wife mean to you?" I inquired. I had
been wondering why a person like Yared wanted to get
married when he already had so much responsibility as
the breadwinner of his family.

"What kind of question is this! Don't you think I am a
man?"

"I know you need a wife as a man. What I am trying
to say is that you are helping your sick mother and your
brothers and sister. Besides, you earn only a few hundreds.
Do you really think marriage is a good idea at this time?"

"You are right in that respect."

"What if you wait until things change for the better?
What is the big hurry?" Then, he told me that his friends
Kassa and Gizaw had encouraged him to ask for my hand.

"Even so, wouldn't it be better for you to propose to
someone with an income?"

"It was not my choice. I just chose you by lot."

Confused, I said, "I don't get you."

He then revealed me how he was forced to propose to me. The three boys selected the three most beautiful girls of the Sunday School and divided the girls among them using the lottery method. The other two girls were Yeshi and Serkalem. I was awarded to Yared. He told me that Yeshi and Serkalem also rejected the proposals of Kassa and Gizaw.

I was happy to hear that they refused.

"Don't you like me?" Yared asked. He looked like a small foolish boy.

I stifled a smile. "I don't hate you."

"Why don't you marry me then?"

I laughed. "What do you mean? I just love you as a sister. And every lover can't be a husband."

He looked depressed.

"I never thought you would feel this way about me." I said after a while. "Our parents act just like a family. I myself considered you as a brother."

"We don't have blood relations, though."

"We are close like a family, anyway."

I arrived home. "Sorry, I just can't help you," I said feeling sorry for him.

I extended my hand to shake his but he was too angry to accept it. He continued walking without uttering a word, leaving me where I was standing.

We didn't see each other for a while and I relaxed, thinking he had forgotten over the matter. But one day he came home in the absence of my parents and resumed nagging me.

"You were Selamawit's boyfriend. Why did you dump her?" I said to him.

"Who told you that?"

"Answer me! What is wrong with Selam?" He couldn't deny his relationship with Selamawit, but refused to tell the reason for their separation. "Tell me why you ditched her?" I insisted. "I know it is Kassa who forced you to leave her, right?"

"He told me that she must be a slut as she accepted my request at once, without hesitation."

I was stunned. "You believed him and ..."

"Who told you all this nonsense?"

Ignoring his question, I said, "First, you just liked her and asked her for friendship. Then, you dumped her because somebody said something bad about her, right?" He nodded.

"You were asking me for friendship. Then, you go to Selamawit. Why?"

"You rejected my proposal."

"Kassa said something about me, right?" I could see that he was shocked. "What did he say about me?"

"Nothing!"

"Don't lie! He told you something bad to make you leave me." He kept silent for a while. "Yared, if you tell me what he told you about me, I will tell you a secret."

"As you hesitated to accept my friendship, Kassa got angry and said you are not as beautiful as Selamawit. He offered to persuade her for me."

"You loved Selamawit, right?"

"Of course, I..."

"But you ignored her lest people think she is a slut because of her swift positive response." He nodded again.

"You have already left me for being ugly. Why do you come back?"

"I thought I made a mistake. You are so nice. I can't stop thinking about you."

"Selamawit is better for you than I am."

"No!"

Yared was led by his friends like water in a canal. He was innocent, shaped and reshaped like a piece of mud in the hands of a potter. I had mixed feelings about him. Sometimes, he irritated me like hell. At times, I felt sorry for him.

"You said you have a secret to tell."

"If I share you the secret, you may quarrel with somebody."

"I won't. Tell me!"

"I can't be sure that you keep the secret," I said looking at him suspiciously.

"I swear."

I paused and reluctantly said, "Your friends have already betrayed you."

"Which of my friends?"

"You know them."

"Kassa and Gizaw?"

"Yes."

"Are you insane? How could my best friends betray me?"

"I am perfectly healthy."

"Ok. What did they do to me?"

"When Selamawit agreed to be your girlfriend, Kassa envied you. He wanted to break your relationship with her by telling you that she is a slut. At the same time, he told her that you don't deserve to be her husband as you are so poor. Then he took Selamawit as his girlfriend."

"Why do you speak this nonsense?"

"I often saw Kassa and Selamawit together. It seemed that they had a special affair. Our classmates talked a lot about it. And I asked Selamawit about it, she did not deny it. You may ask someone else, if you don't believe me."

"You don't mean it?" His small eyes went out of their sockets.

"Yes. Now Selamawit is his girlfriend. Maybe he will ditch her after a while. You can check it for yourself. Remember what he had said to you when he wanted you to quit me. By the way, both Gizaw and Kassa were asking me to have sex with them."

He said, "This is unbelievable!" But I could see that he was realizing that he had been cheated by his friends.

"Dear brother Yared, let me give you a piece of advice. Kassa and Gizaw are not good friends. Don't trust them. It's too early for you to think about marriage! Concentrate on improving your livelihood for now..."

"Let me see those sons of bitches!" He roared with rage. "I know what to do with them! I will teach those dogs a lesson. I will throw them into the river!" He was furious.

I became worried about his health and state of mind.

"You promised me you would not quarrel with anybody, remember?"

"I am YARED! The son of ...!" He rushed out of the house as angry as a wounded leopard.

Chapter 14

I was able to relax a bit as the boys left me alone for a while. But Father would not leave me alone. He continued to nag me to marry the wealthy merchant, Aychew. One evening when he must have been drinking, he shouted, "I said you should get married, period!"

"I told you that I don't want to marry him." I felt sick. I was tired of this discussion.

"I am the one who decides." He stared at me angrily with his bloodshot eyes.

"You are not living my life, though," I shouted back.

"I can't sit legs crossed when you forgot your fortune."

"I can achieve more if I continue studying."

"Better life has nothing to do with hard work and mere education. You are not a good student even if you love the idea of being educated."

"Just give me some time and you will see."

"You better bear your own children and send them to school."

"I have ample time for that."

"You will marry the man. It is cut and dried!"

"I don't want to marry anybody!"

"What you wish doesn't matter, but my decision matters."

He told me the date he had set for the wedding.

"Don't waste your money for the wedding. I will never marry somebody I hardly know," I said.

"We will see," he replied gnashing his teeth.

I knew that the only reason my father told me the wedding date was because I was at school studying. When the girls in the rural areas are wedded, their wedding day is often kept from them for the reason some girls may run away to avoid getting married. Her parents don't take her to the tailor. They secretly take one of her dresses to the tailor to show her size. They lie to her about the food and drinks preparation saying that they are celebrating a religious festival. On her wedding day, they lock her in a room until the bridegroom comes. Only then she would know. When I heard that my wedding day was decided, I was shocked. I was very sorry with my father for his stubbornness to decide my fate on his own without my consent even if I had been seriously opposing him whenever he raised the idea of marriage. But soon I thought I was lucky to be told the date of my wedding day.

I was very angry. "Am I to fill somebody's gap? Shouldn't I strive for my own life? Is a girl created just to marry and bear children? Who decides the fate of a girl?" I screamed.

"What is your goal?"

"Just to get educated, get some kind of employment"

"Know yourself. Do you think you can do that?"

"I can."

"'Morning shows a day' as the saying goes"

"What do you mean?"

"I know how you are doing at school."

"Don't worry about it. If you persist in giving me away to somebody through family arranged marriage, I will sue you."

"What did you say? Say it again!" He looked me in the eye.

"I will sue you!" I shouted.

"Really?" he asked in disbelief. "That is great. What a heroine you are! I bet you can do it!"

"Things have changed now. There are a lot of organizations working for the rights of women. All I have to do is to inform them about my situation. I can even inform my teachers."

"What do you think they would do?"

"They may take to the street demonstrating against you. Then they will sue you."

"If you do so, do you think I would take you as my child?"

"Believe me. I will do it!"

"Only a fool does as he is told."

The next day, I left the classroom during the recess and sat alone. I didn't want to play with friends since I was very depressed. I couldn't attend class attentively.

Gizaw saw me and came up to me. "How are you, girl?" he said.

"Are you greeting me or provoking me?"

"Whatever you think about it."

"What has brought you here?"

"My legs."

"Leave me alone."

"You want me to go?"

"If you don't mind..."

"Are you scared someone would tell Aychew?"

"Who is Aychew?"

"You think we didn't hear anything. We know about everything." He smiled proudly.

My father used to be careful not to hurt my feelings. That was why he took me out for a walk to convince me to marry Aychew. But he no more cared after some time. He of course strictly warned my siblings not to tell anybody about his decision. I wondered from where Gizaw got the information. I was not happy that he knew.

"What are you talking about?"

"About the two of you, you and Aychew."

"Are you crazy?" I was annoyed.

"No, I am not."

"If not, why are you nagging me?"

"Are you angry because I know about it?"

"Mind your words. Otherwise, I am going to sue you for insulting me."

I left him alone and rushed to my classroom. He followed after me.

"It is shameful that you are to be Aychew's while you rejected us pretending that you want to finish your education."

"For one thing I am not getting married. Even so, I don't see any problem." I said trying hard to calm myself down.

"It is a shame."

"What is there to be ashamed of?"

"Money is the source of evil."

"That's not the right quotation."

"Correct me, Emu," he said sarcastically.

I stared at him and said to him, "You are a wolf in a sheep's skin. You betrayed your innocent friend."

"Oh really? How about jilting a lover for money?" Gizaw said.

"I don't have a lover in the first place."

"I know Yared was yours. I too fell in love with you...."

"Oh, do you mean it?" I said to him mockingly. "Do you know anything about love?"

I saw a flash of anger in his eyes. He said, "You are cruel."

"I am lucky!" I entered my classroom.

Chapter 15

I kept on studying hard. I even studied with passion this time, envisioning a better future as an educated woman. I gave up the habit of yawning while reading my text books and became a voracious reader, often spending the entire night reading exposed to the smoke of the kerosene lantern. I rarely play with the family. When I was not studying, I worried that I was wasting time. The change within me was indeed surprising.

I faced on big hurdle to continuing my education. My father was not likely to provide the money I needed to continue my high school education in the nearby Gimjjabet town, which was located twenty-seven kilometers away from Ayehu. My father was the one who would decide whether to let me continue studying or not.

Subjects delivered in English language were difficult for me. My parents couldn't assist me as they had dropped out from eighth grade. I was the oldest and most educated member of the family. As a result, I usually went to teacher's home for help. While doing some errands for

Teacher Abeba, I relied on her generous support. I made a relentless effort in improving my competence in English language. Teacher Abeba always congratulated me on the significant change I had made in my study habits. I didn't believe her, though. I remained unsatisfied. I still worried whether I would be able to stand on my own in the world or not.

One day, while we were playing during the school recess, one of the boys pointed his finger at me and said, "She would join one of the colleges, believe me!" The attention of the students shifted towards me.

"She may join one of the colleges, alright but ..." the second boy left the sentence unfinished.

"What bother you then?" said Gizaw.

"I am afraid she may get crazy after such a hard work!"

"That could happen," said the fourth boy.

"...she is trying to do what others do..."

"What a pity there is no one advising her on what to do."

I rushed out of the classroom, being upset by their discussion.

"Don't expose yourself to the sun too much. What if your knowledge just evaporates after studying hard...?"

Students who ridicule me were increasing from day to day, but Gizaw went too far.

Teacher Abeba, overhearing what was being said about me, said, "Don't listen to those who are telling you negative things. Don't worry at all about what they say."

I did my best to avoid boys like Kassa and Gizaw by staying away from the church's social services. I gave them different reasons for my absence. I told them that I was very busy cooking, washing and other domestic activities. In fact, I was studying all the time. One Saturday, my friends got tired of hearing my pretexts, came to my house, and began nagging me for not taking part in their social activities. Gizaw was the head of the delegation.

"There is no one who becomes fat by shunning fasting; and there is no one who becomes wealthy by violating Holy days." Gizaw said.

"The quote is not appropriate. It doesn't describe me." I got furious.

"It is appropriate indeed! You are refusing to take part in any activity. You were very eager to do such things before. What is new today? What are you planning to do?" I got angrier than ever.

"Are you telling me to abandon my studying and helping my mother?"

"We indeed study and help our respective mothers. What is so unique about you?" a girl named Hirut commented.

"Besides, I want to avoid them as well." I said pointing at Gizaw and Kassa.

"What did we do to you?" Kassa demanded to know.

"I don't like what you are up to."

"What is that supposed to mean?"

"We the girls were coming to church to worship God but you are trying to woo us."

"You must be insane!" Kassa exclaimed.

"Shunning the Sunday School cannot be good!" Gizaw said.

The delegation was shocked by my reaction, especially, Gizaw and Kassa who were very upset. I did not care. "Look," I said."I will never come to church so long as the two of you are in the Sunday School. I wish you never call me again. Is that clear?"

I left my own house and went to a neighbor's until they left my home.

Chapter 16

My father couldn't quit hoping that I would marry the businessman one day. One day I had had enough of it.

"Father!"

"Yes, my girl!"

"I know I am a burden to you..."

"I didn't say so."

"Yes, I am. Allow me to leave..."

"To go where?"

"Anywhere my legs take me, to another town or to a monastery."

"I want you to get married for your sake." He looked sad.

"You are hurting me. Such a marriage will never survive. It won't last even for two weeks."

"How can you tell that?"

"I can't live a stable life without completing my education. I prefer to die."

"You know my salary. How can I send you to town with this income?"

"Just leave me alone. God will help me in continuing my education. After all, I can educate myself being employed as a housemaid."

"Mengist, why don't you leave her alone?" said my mother, who said nothing so far about my marriage. She must have been scared of my leaving for good. I was happy to have my mother's support. I gave full attention to my education. My relationship with the family improved remarkably.

My improvement in my lessons was steady. I, who never stood better than fortieth in any class, stood thirty-third out of sixty-five students in the first semester of eighth grade, and seventeenth in the second semester. My parents were surprised with my scores.

In fact, the improvement was a result of Teacher Abeba's efforts as she was buying reference books for me, tutoring me, and advising me on how to study my lessons. Gradually, I was able to understand how to take notes from reference books. My fluency and accuracy in English language improved as well.

Sometimes, I said to myself, *Poor Emebet! You are not born to be scholar,* and I felt low.

I told Teacher Abeba how I felt. She read me a sentence from a book entitled *You Can Win* which was the saying of an Italian painter and sculptor, Michael Angelo. Angelo said, "If people knew how hard I had to work to gain my mastery, it wouldn't seem wonderful at all."

Teacher Abeba continued, "Be sure about success. It will eventually come to you because you are in the right track. Keep it up. What is expected of you is to scale up your effort towards success." She was always optimistic, and she was also sensitive when telling someone of their shortcomings. I was so lucky to have her as a teacher and a friend too.

When I got my results of the eighth grade examination and saw I had passed, I was so happy to be promoted. I was afraid that if I failed to be promoted from eighth grade, my father would be angry and use it as support for his argument about why I should get married. I showed my father the report card. He glanced at it and gave it back to me.

"Oh, Father!" I stared at him, surprised.

"You better listen to my advice."

"No, Father. No," I said shaking my head.

"You'll regret it one day."

"I won't."

* * *

Two weeks later, I went by bus to Gimjjabet. The gravel road to the town was in a bad shape, full of potholes. The bus creaked as it moved up the gentle slope to Gimjjabet. I had expected that my father would go in advance to rent a room. But it was my mother who did that. He did not even come to the bus terminal to see me off. In fact, he gave me the money I needed.

"Now the issue of Aychew is a thing of the past," I thought. Aychew would despair now that I would be out of my parents' sight. He also might know that Kassa and Gizaw were hovering over me.

Chapter 17

G imjjabet is situated at a high altitude. It has a cold climate with a lot of rain which was a big change for me since Ayehu is known for its hot climate and rampant malaria. There is no malaria in Gimjjabet because of the high altitude. The town is bigger than Ayehu with a round clock electric service and a bank and it is lovelier than Ayehu. Even though its roads are dusty like Ayehu's and they are full of potholes, they don't get muddy despite the heavy rains as the red dust of the road is sandy. Most homes had electric light, which was a great help for my study.

The first thing I did on arriving in Gimjjabet was to look for a good female student to be friend with. School was difficult. Classes in the Gimjjabet High School were taught using a Plasma TV. We students sat in class and watched an instructor on the TV. We had to make notes on our own and we could not ask the teacher on the TV to stop or slow down. I found this difficult and wanted to become friends with another serious student who could work with me to overcome these difficulties. Eventually, I met with Yekaba, a girl from Buya Eyesus. I shared a desk with Yekaba. One day our Chemistry teacher was absent and I began correcting my notes by comparing them with hers.

"The teachers on the plasma TV teach too quickly and I can't understand them," I said.

"Yes, we all have that problem," Yekaba replied.

"It was better when teachers wrote notes on the black board."

"Yesterday, a boy asked one of the teachers to write on the blackboard."

I had not attended the class the day before.

"What did the teacher say?"

"He said, `Spoon feeding has come to an end, this is not elementary school.'"

I couldn't keep up with the teachers on the plasma TV. When I tried to write fast, it was hard even for me to read my hand writing. I hated the plasma but I did not have any alternative except to get used to it.

After a month, I went home to Ayehu to bring food. I met Yared at the bus station. He greeted me warmly. He carried my baggage although I insisted that he shouldn't. We began strolling toward home together.

"How is school?"

"It is fine."

"Is it not difficult?"

"It is okay."

"Great!" He was happy for me.

After a while, we talked about Kassa and Gizaw, "The two devils" we called them.

"I heard Kassa is visiting you."

"No."

"Don't lie to me" he said looking in my eyes.

"What for?" In fact, while Gizaw was my schoolmate and studying with me, Kassa, who had left high school long ago, was coming to Gimjjabet for different purposes.

"How about Gizaw? Is he bothering you?"

"He has already given up bothering me," I replied.

He relaxed.

He paused and hesitantly asked, "How about the two of us?"

"I thought it is over."

"I think we have an unfinished business."

"I don't think so. It's over. You can't force me to marry you, can you?"

"If you are to marry either Gizaw or Kassa, you will be as good as dead," he said knitting his brow.

"What do you mean?"

"I will kill both of you." He sounded determined.

"Do you think you can live in peace after committing murder?"

"Who is to touch me?"

"You would go to jail and spend half of your life time there."

"They need to catch me first."

"Can you bury yourself underground?"

"Sudan is just here." He said pointing westward with his chin towards the Sudanese border.

"Are you going to touch it?" I said laughing.

"I am not joking." He didn't smile at all.

I laughed. "I can see you are serious," I said sarcastically.

"Well, you will see!"

It seems Yared is as angry as ever.

We got nearer to my home.

"Aren't you coming in?"

"What for?"

"We can have tea. You can also have a meal."

"You are a guest, too. You don't know what is available in the house after staying away from home."

"There will be enough for the two of us."

"Do you exercise witch-crafting?" he said grinning and handing my baggage over.

I giggled. "It is not so. Mother knows I am coming home today."

"Oh, really? First, eat well yourself and have your fill," he said.

"Thank you, anyway." I said.

"For what?"

"For helping me with the baggage and for the warning"

"Don't joke with me."

"I am not joking."

He headed to his home. I didn't go into my home. I looked at him from behind and felt sorry for him though I don't know why. I thought of him as an orphan. I compared his straight and open nature with that of Kassa and Gizaw's. What a difference!

Mother was not at home yet so Sossina served me supper. I ate well. After meal, she said, "I am going back to work."

"I can help you."

"No, get some rest. You can help us tomorrow." I was left alone.

Sossina will take the grade eight Ministry of Education Examamination which is given to all eight graders across Ethiopia. She was not paying attention to her education as she had to help mother with the household chores. While

I was in Gimjjabet I wrote a letter advising her about her career. I had planned to discuss in depth about her fate with mother.

Kassa came to visit as soon as Sossina entered our kitchen.

"Welcome home, Emebet," he said.

"Amen!" I was not happy to see him.

"How do you do?"

"I'm fine."

He said, "You are very talkative."

"Thanks!"

"Why can't you keep a secret?"

I stared at him angrily. "You didn't warn me to do so."

"Even so, you should know what to tell and what not. You are a traitor!"

"Why are you insulting me?"

"You know what you said to Yared."

"What about that?"

"What is the point of telling him such nonsense?"

I kept silent.

"What is said between two persons should be a secret. What we discussed shouldn't have been told to Yared."

"He would know it sooner or later. It is not a secret as such."

"Why not?"

"You proposed me right? If so, Yared would know it eventually"

"It is possible to hide the information from him."

"How?"

"We can flee the country."

"Really? I shall leave my parents, brother and sisters and my birthplace just for the sake of your happiness?" I was angered by his selfish behavior.

"It is something to be paid for love."

"I will never love you,"

He continued blaming me, ignoring what I said.

"You committed an unpardonable crime. He threatened to kill me. Don't do this again!"

"Okay, sir."

"Don't tease me. Had he done something to me, I would have avenged you."

"Leave me alone. My parents will come any time. Besides, Yared would be mad at you if he knows you were here"

"What can he do?"

"He would flog you like a child."

"Would my hands be tied when he flogged me?"

"Go away. Don't boast!"

I knew he was disappointed because I praised Yared. He stared at me and said, "You are challenging me, huh? I am not foolish."

"Please go! I don't want the two of you to fight over me."

He was angry. On the contrary, I was satisfied.

He took a deep breath and said, "You better not act this way." He then left.

Chapter 18

I showed my first semester result to Teacher Abeba. "Take five!" she exclaimed. We shook hands. She shook me for long as a token of appreciation. She hugged me until I felt pain in my breasts. She scrutinized the answer sheets all over again. She couldn't believe how well I had done.

"I was dying to see this day," she said. I said nothing. I scored more than thirty points out of forty marks in all but one subject over forty-five points out of sixty. It is a stunning success for a student like me who had not been doing well for most of her life in school.

"Look what you were able to achieve in less than two years," she was impressed with my scores. I scanned the papers again. Teacher Abeba entered into the living room and began searching for something. She uncovered an agenda notebook and began scribbling in it. I read the writing it said, "Emuye, you are the designer of your destiny. You are the author. You write the story. The pen is in your hand. And the outcome is whatever you choose."

"You are the author of your history. You can be what you are aspiring for. You can strengthen or weaken yourself.

You have begun restoring your name. After a while no one would know that you were weak in academic affairs. You can be sure about that," she reiterated emotionally. She got excited.

"What do you want to be in the future?" she asked me with a serious concern.

"I want to be a medical doctor."

"You can be if you want it so badly," she asserted. After reading the two books, *the Diary of Anne Frank* and *You Can Win*, I usually contemplated having a trade that would satisfy my ego. I don't want my life history to read like, "She was born in...married to... bore such and such children...and died on ..." I wanted to have an eternal name and a sacred soul.

I recalled those people who were able to change the world for the better. Michael Faraday, Thomas Edison, the Wright, Lewis Pastor, Sir Isaac Newton, Alexander Graham Bell, mother Teresa, ...to mention a few. I envied them. I promised to do something special to live in people's mind for eternity. I would study even harder!

Teacher Abeba gave me the agenda notebook as a gift. She also shared some quotes from "The Secret". She said the book had changed her life for the better. I had improved my school results but that was not quite enough.

Chapter 19

I returned to school in Gimjjabet.

One day Kassa came to the town. He waited for me at the school gate. I was talking to Yekaba and did not see him until he called out to me. I asked Yekaba to wait for me and walked over to where he stood.

"What is going on? Are you okay?" I asked him

"I am not ok. I'm head over heels in love with."

"Who is she?"

"You, who else?"

"You must be kidding?" I chuckled.

"It is you who is kidding, not me." He sounded serious.

"Wait. How many girls should you love at once?"

"I love only one girl and that is you."

"How about Selamawit?"

"You buda, evil-eyed!"

"Don't worry. I won't devour someone like you." He got angry with my reply as he is not a good looking guy. His behavior is worse than that.

"Who told you that Selamawit is mine?"

"Were you thinking that it would remain secret?"

"Women never keep secrets."

"Men are worse."

"Let's drop this topic…"

"Well. Why do you jilt her?"

"It is not I jilted her…" he left the sentence unfinished.

"And?"

"Women always go to the haves."

"Are you telling me that she betrayed you?"

"It is saddening, isn't it?"

"Selam will never do this. You must have offended her."

"You can say whatever!"

"You separated her from Yared while you know you would jilt her, right?"

"It is not me who separated the two. It is she who changed her mind."

"You think I know nothing about it?" He kept quiet. "Why do you come to me now?"

"I couldn't forget you."

"There is a saying that goes like this, 'A fox spends the whole day expecting that a bull's scrotum will fall eventually.'"

"Don't do that to me."

"Excuse me for saying that. It explains your situation." I hurried to Yekaba who is waiting for me. I didn't want Kassa to know where I lived so I headed to Yekaba's dormitory. Kassa did not follow me.

I thought Kassa would leave me alone for good but he behaved like a dog that has no integrity. I insulted him and Yared threatened him but to no avail, he persisted in visiting me. One day, he came to my dormitory.

"What do you want from me?' I was very angry at him.

"I came to Kosober town to look for a vacancy. I missed the bus to Ayehu."

"Why do you come here?" I was still mad at him.

"I didn't have supper."

I served him supper assuming that he may not have money. After dinner, I told him to leave the house.

"I have no place to go," he said blinking his eyes.

"You may go to your friends."

"How about spending the night here with you?"

"That is not possible!"

"Why?"

"I have only one bed."

"How about sharing it?"

I stared at him. To my surprise, he was not smiling at all.

"How can a girl spend the night with a man who is not her husband?"

"What is the problem?"

"You know what the problem is," I snapped.

"I only come to you because I couldn't find Gizaw."

"Why don't you rent a bedroom?"

"All the bedrooms are already occupied."

"So you are planning to spend the night here?" I couldn't believe what he was saying to me.

"I will leave early in the morning so as not to tarnish your name."

"Thank you for being thoughtful. Wait for me," I knew a resident in the premises called Hibret. She was a single woman working as an agricultural development agent.

"May I bother you for a day? I want to spend the night with you as a guest has occupied my bedroom."

"It is okay," she agreed. I returned to my dormitory, picked my nightwear, and left the padlock to my unwelcomed guest on the table. "You can lock the house if you leave early tomorrow," I said keeping the key with me.

"How about spending the night together?" He smiled lustfully.

"What you need is a bed, right?"

"I would be happy if we could spend the night talking about our childhood."

"How come a fire be with benzene? You would bet tempted. "

"I have never been tempted with sister like you."

"You have already been tempted when you come to me"

"No. I come here because I have no place to spend the night."

"It is just a pretext."

"Believe me. It is the truth!" I left the room.

"Okay. I can go to friends. You don't need to leave your dormitory." He followed after me outside.

"Didn't you say they are not around?"

"No." He scratched his head. "I know where they are. I just want to spend the night with you."

"If that is the case, you better go to your friends. I shouldn't trouble my neighbor."

I returned to the room. He sat on a stool and made no motions as if he was planning to leave. Understanding that he would never leave me alone, I said, "Be my guest for today." I went to Hibret's to spend the night.

He followed me and announced, "The house is not locked. You come back and lock it!"

My landlord overheard him and approached, demanding to know why he was there.

Kassa kept silent.

"I am speaking to you. What are you doing here?" The landlord was holding a stick for self-defense.

"Don't look at me like that. What do I do to you?" Kassa retorted.

"It is not time for a man to come to a girl. Get out of here," the landlord shouted.

Kassa rushed towards the main gate. The owner followed him and waited, standing at the gate, to make sure Kassa left. After locking my dormitory, I spent the night at Hibret's lest Kassa may come back.

In the next day, Kassa was waiting for me at the gate of the school. "You gave me to the hyenas, right?"

"You were not short of friends."

"I have been suffering from your love for years. But you don't have the slightest sympathy for me."

"Kassa, I am out of patience. Get out of here before I cry for help!"

"You won't do that unless you are out of your mind."

"I have no time. Be off!" He stood in front of me like a pole blocking my way.

"Well, I will call for help if you can take the risk?" Our dialogue attracted the attention of the students entering the school compound. Some of them seemed to be irritated by his presence. This encouraged me even further. While I was at the verge of attacking him with one of my shoes, he side-stepped a little and stood there.

Chapter 20

G iven my great effort, I got promoted to tenth grade with good marks. But I couldn't get someone to tutor me during the summer since teachers left Ayehu to their parents or summer courses. Teacher Abeba also left for Bahir Dar for her own studies.

I spent the summer studying the exercise books of former tenth grade students. This helped me to revise previous courses of ninth grade. I also formed friendship with Yekaba, who turned out to be not only intelligent but also humble and honest. We began studying together, and after some time, we started living in the same dormitory.

We took the examinations. I was very nervous about my performance. I knew I had done better than ever, but I couldn't be sure I had done well in comparison to all the tenth grade students of the country. I wanted to continue my education by joining one of the preparatory schools, but to do that I needed a certain minimum grade. Once I got that opportunity, going to college would be easier for me.

I was already back in Ayehu when the results were announced at last. Mother wanted to go to Gimjjabet with me but I declined.

"I would do anything to see my daughter's results," she said. I knew she was worried about my wellbeing if my results were unsatisfactory.

"You don't have to go all the way to Gimjjabet," I said.

"Don't waste your energy in persuading me to stay here," she responded firmly. We met Teacher Abeba at Gimjjabet waiting a public transport to Ayehu. She hugged and kissed me as soon as she saw me. She was overjoyed.

"My dear heroin," the teacher said tears flooding her cheeks. I stood there speechless. All of a sudden, mother started ululating. The teacher told me right away that I scored 3.2 Cummulative Grade Point Average. It was out of 4.00. My friend, Yekaba scored 3.5. I was so happy I wanted to jump for joy.

"Thanks to God I passed this exam. I know what to do next time!" I vowed to myself. However, Teacher Abeba responded right away, "You are lucky. I am transferred from Ayehu to Gimjjabet this year."

"Oh, that is great!" I screamed with excitement. My tears cascaded down to my chin. Mother said nothing except mentioning that I was so lucky.

I started the lessons in eleventh grade with great morale and eagerness. Yekaba and I found a room in our dormitory for Teacher Abeba. We did errands for her and she tutored us. The rest of the teachers also helped us in our lessons.

My lessons became less and less difficult. I understood the subjects easily as I had been improving my competence in the English language. I was promoted to grade 12 standing fourth in the class and Yekaba stood second. It boosted my morale even higher than ever.

I understood that I had very little time for preparations for entrance exam to higher learning institutions. The work was very hard and sometimes I wished I was still at eleventh grade. I studied day and night. I was dying to see those persons who used to tell me that I was useless, to hear them say, "We were wrong."

I always imagined myself treating people suffering from various illnesses. Patients would say, "Thanks, I feel better now." I exerted a lot of effort to reach to my planned destination. Now I feel that I can achieve it.

Chapter 21

Sometimes, Yāred came to Gimjjabet and visited me. I thought he was coming to the town as a stopover when he came for his own affairs. My negative view towards him had changed. I worried about him and cared about what happened to him. First, I thought it was because he lost his mother; but I understood the feeling to be beyond that later. There was something attractive about him. He was not sly like his friends.

One morning he came to visit me on his way back to Ayehu. He sat on a stool. I gave him a glass of tea and bread and sat on the egde of my bed.

"I had been angry with you. But now I have forgotten it," I said.

"Why?"

"Because you sent your friends to me. Why didn't you talk to me yourself?"

"I feel nervous in front of the girl I love. I came twice but couldn't tell you my feelings."

I laughed. "You're talking to me right now."

"Now you know my feelings well. I don't feel nervous anymore."

I wished he had told me his feelings himself stammering and sweating with fear in front of me.

"But why?" I asked myself. And the answer was clear, "It's because I love him."

"It's not time to think about love." I rebuked myself.

One day, he told me that he was coming to Gimjjabet only to see me.

"Why do you take the trouble of coming this far?"

"You women love to see us suffering."

"Yared, you are suffering for nothing."

"I can't live without you. I just can't!"

"For one thing, you have already been living without me until this day. For another, there are numerous girls much more beautiful than I am..."

"Yes. But I can't continue this way, not anymore."

"How come you let yourself love me when I told you some years back that I could not marry you?"

"I don't know why. After you rejected my proposal, I lost interest in life. I even prayed to God to take my life."

"No! Why should you die for me when there are lots of beautiful girls around?" I said deeply shocked by what he said.

"I don't know. I always think bad things."

"Selamawit, who is more beauty than I am, was your girlfriend. You jilted her. As for me, it is better for you to abandon the notion of marriage for a time being and improve your livelihood. If you insist in getting married, you better get married to a girl dropped out of tenth grade and who has no ambition to continue studying. Don't contemplate dying like a fool," I advised him.

"Sorry, I don't want to see your failure, but will you marry me if you failed to join a university?"

"If I am to marry, I shall marry a man who would let me live a decent life. Don't mistake me for a fortune-hunter as your friends used to describe me. I just don't want to marry a man with no trade and destine my children to suffer from the hands of poverty. My goal is to live a decent life. I don't care what others say about it."

"Do you think I will remain poor throughout my life? Am I incapable of improving my livelihood?"

"If you are determined to change your life for the better, God will help you for sure. However, God would do nothing to people who have no vision. After all, you need to have something to be blessed by God."

"In short, you are telling me that you don't have an interest in being mine?"

"I don't want to think about marriage at this time."

"I am so sorry."

"Had you stayed with Selamawit still now, the separation would have come from her. Kassa told her about your economic status. No girl wants to lead a miserable life. Therefore, improve your livelihood first before aspiring to have a wife."

"How can I do that in absence of money, land of my own, and without educating myself?"

"There are people who create miracles from situations worse than yours. You can change your life for the better."

"It is not as easy as you think it is," he said.

"Yared, both poverty and wealth are in your hands. You can be either poor or wealthy. But if you think your situation will never change, it will be as you wish. You can win poverty if you want to. You can make your poverty history. Believe me!"

"You are right. But how can a man aspire for a better life while he has nothing for a start."

"It is easy if you are keen to be changed."

"Can you show me how?"

"Sure."

"Tell me then," he said with eagerness.

"You have a capacity to be a runner, an athlete. You won many school competitions, remember? You can be a renowned athlete within two to three years. By then, it is women who would strive to marry you, not the other way round." I smiled.

"I will begin exercising right away, thanks for your showing me the way." He shook my hand and left with high spirit.

Within a year, Yared's name began to appear in the list of winning athletes in domestic races.

After completion of twelfthgrade, I scored 560 points out of 700 in the E.S.L.C.E. and joined Gonder University in order to study Medical Science.Yared, who became famous day by day, also began participating in international competitions.